YORICK AND BÖNES

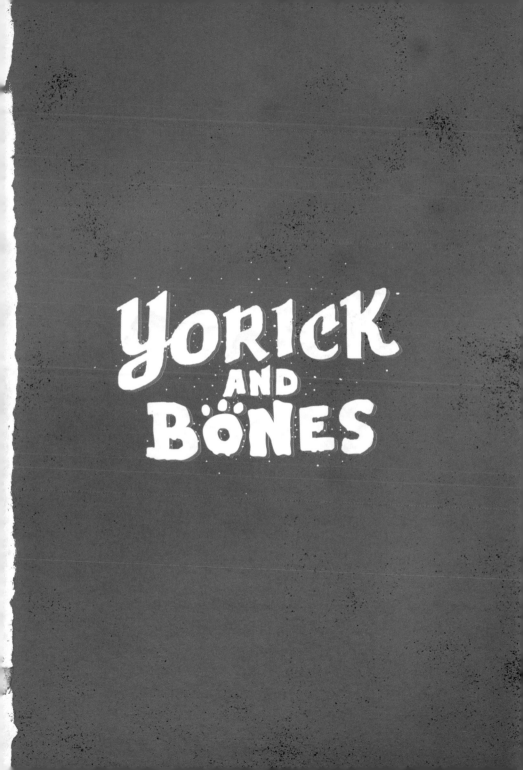

YORICK AND BÖNES

JEREMY TANKARD AND HERMIONE TANKARD

HARPER alley

An Imprint of HarperCollinsPublishers

HarperAlley is an imprint of HarperCollins Publishers.

Yorick and Bones

For information address HarperCollins Children's Books, a division of HarperCollins Publishers, 195 Broadway, New York, NY 10007.
www.harperalley.com
Library of Congress Control Number: 2019939423
ISBN 978-0-06-285430-8 — ISBN 978-0-06-285431-5 (paperback)
The artist used Clip Studio to create the digital illustrations for this book.
Typography by Chris Dickey
20 21 22 23 24 SCP 10 9 8 7 6 5 4 3 2 1
❖
First Edition

Jeremy: For Hermione, of course!

Hermione: For my mom and dad, and for my friends.
You guys make nerdiness cool!

ACT ONE:
LOVE BITES

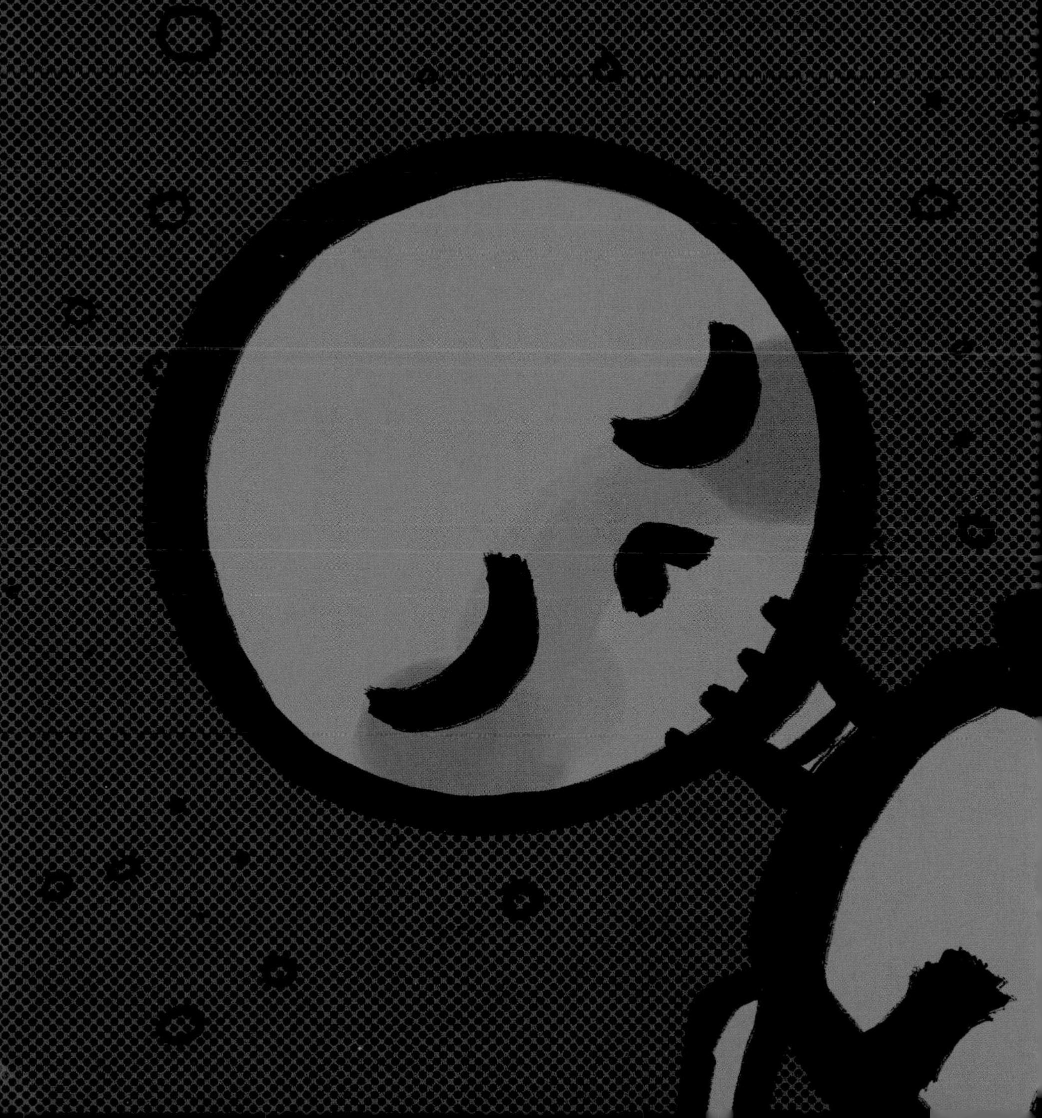

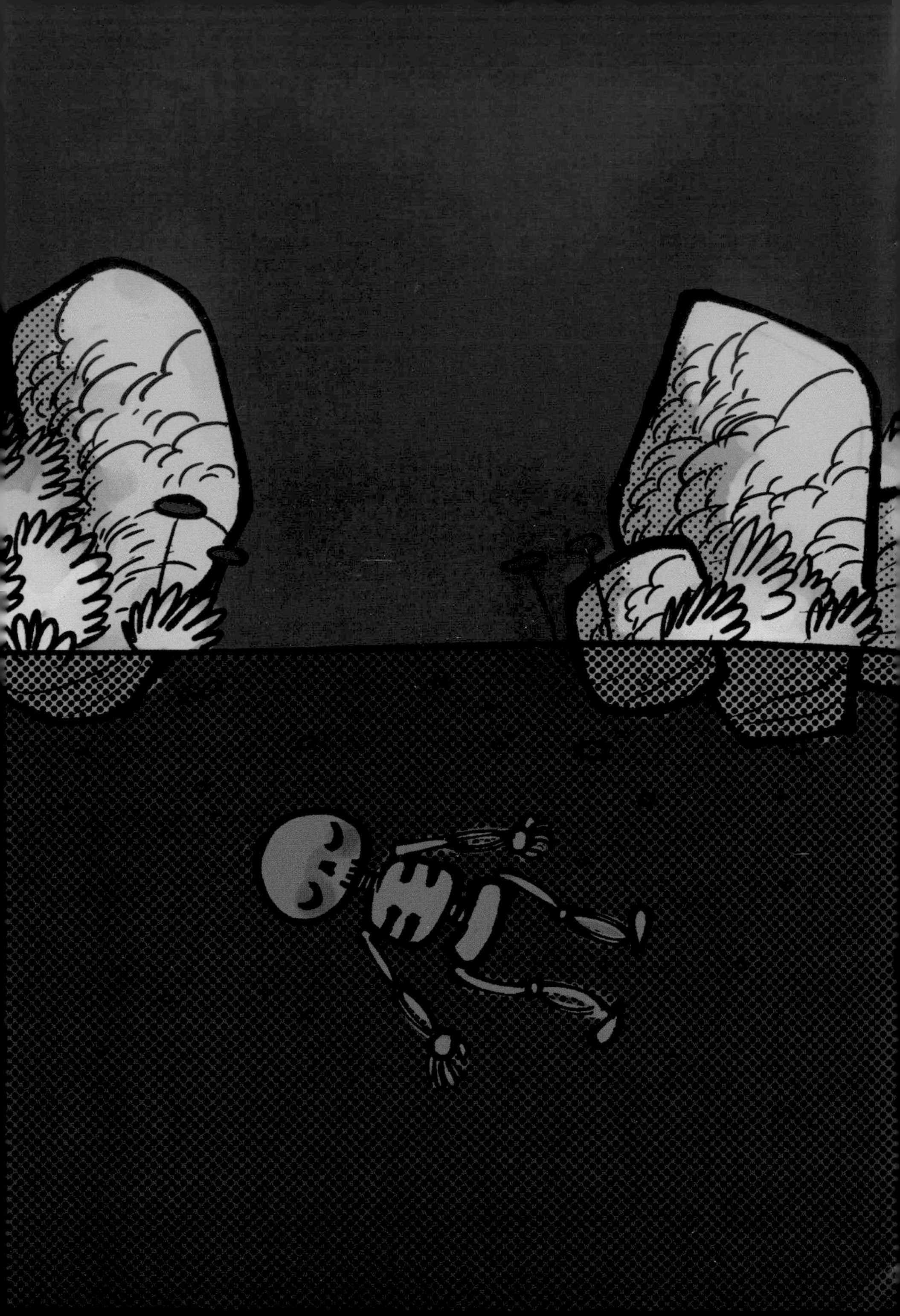

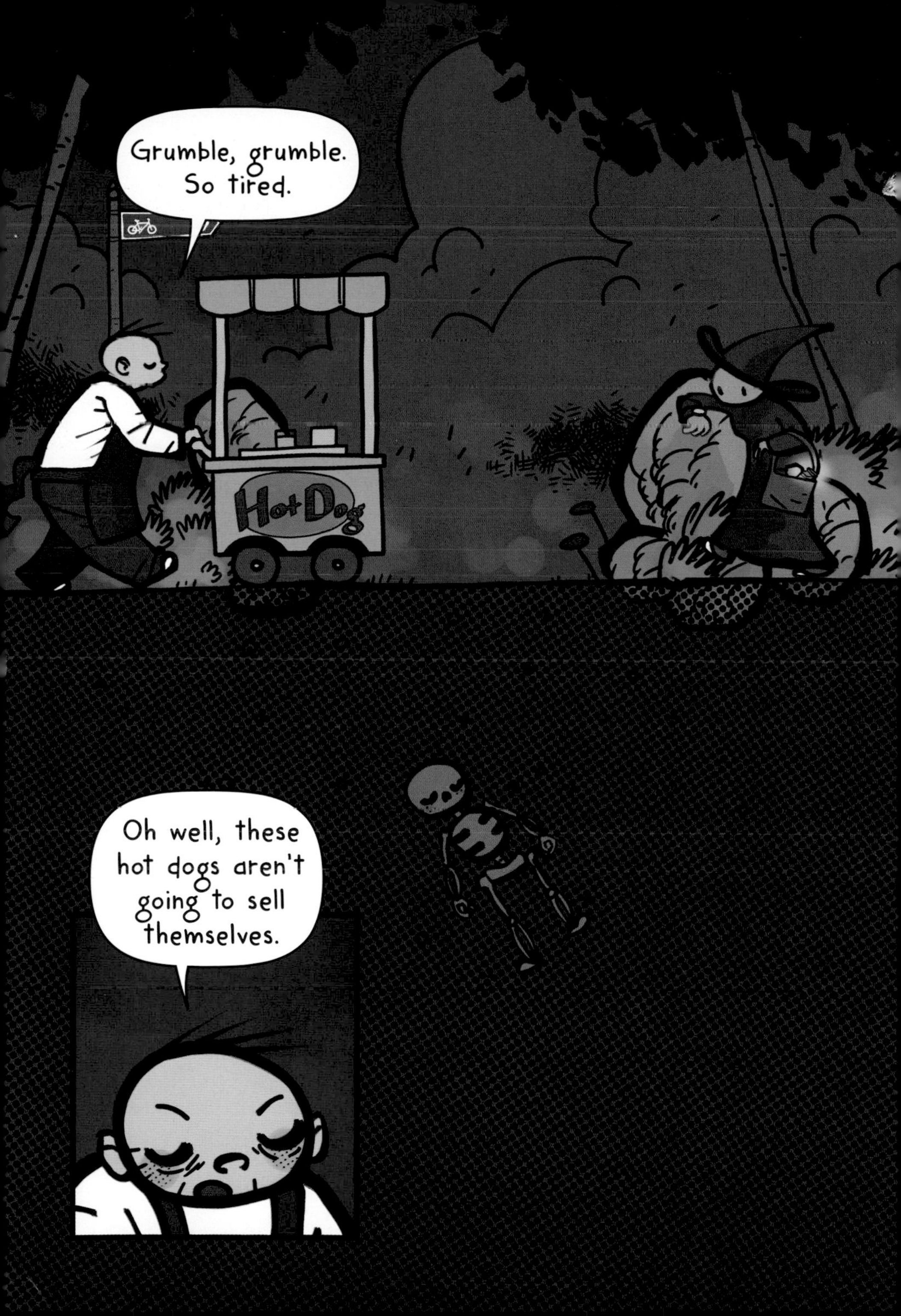
Grumble, grumble. So tired.
Hot Dog
Oh well, these hot dogs aren't going to sell themselves.

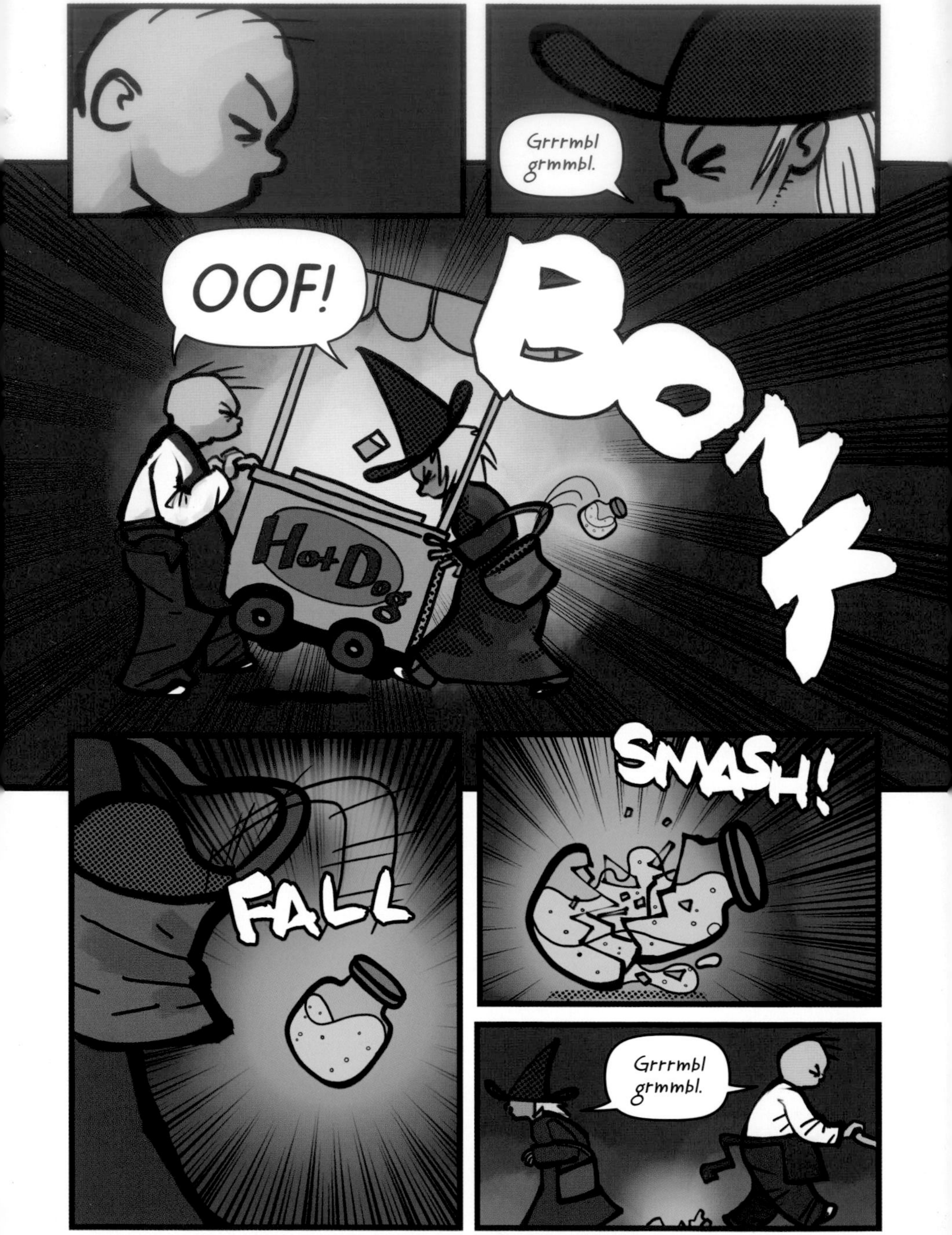
Grrrmbl grmmbl.
OOF!
BONK
FALL
SMASH!
Grrrmbl grmmbl.

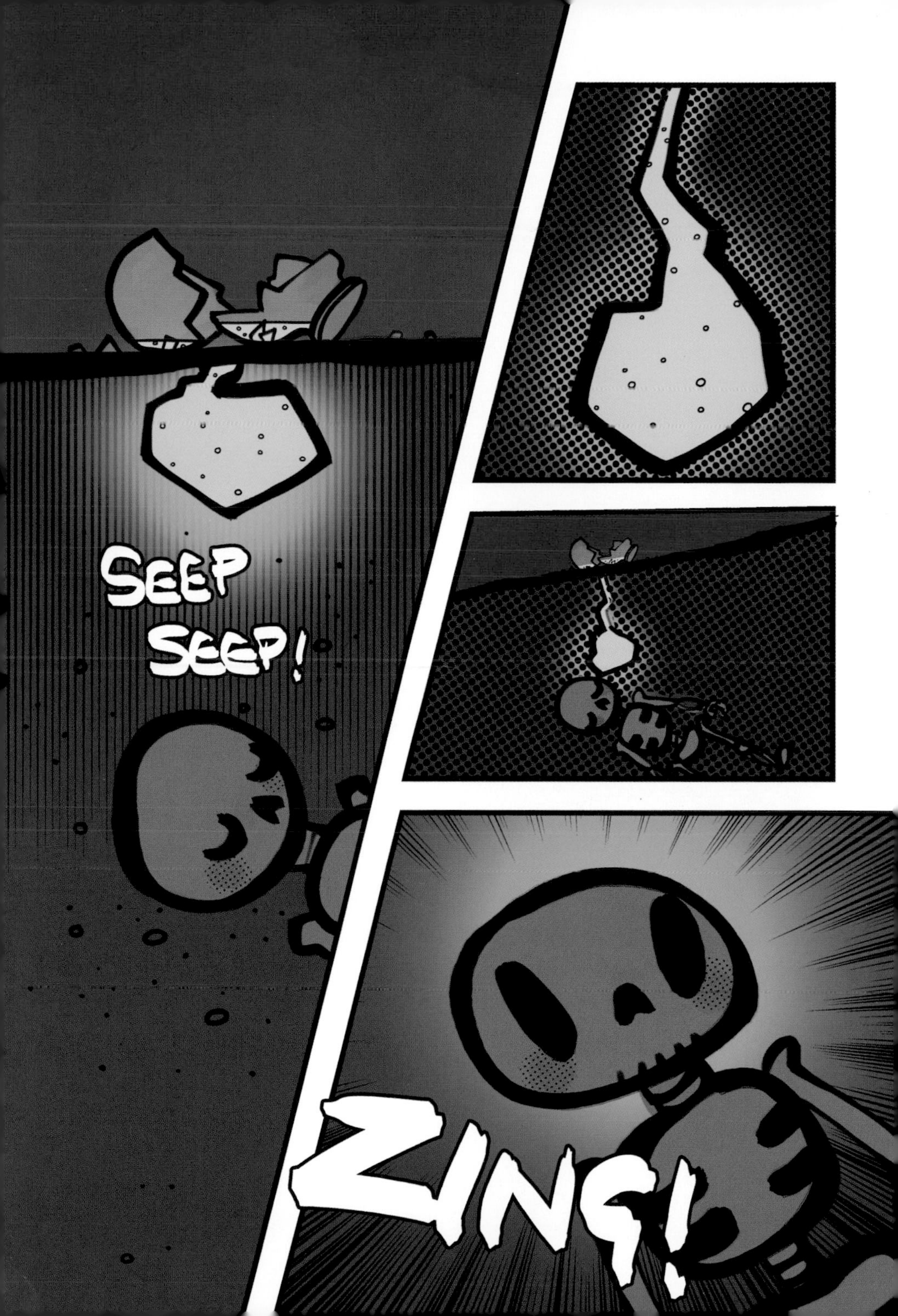
SEEP
SEEP!
ZING!

Alas! Once more? I would I were asleep!
Whenever my eyes doth open it is dark! It seems eternity that I have slept; So long I nary can recall my past.
Oh, did I hide in jest and not be found?
Or did I lie and sleep beneath cool shade?
Nay, that can't be, for now I find I am All cover'd o'er with heavy, damp, dark soil.

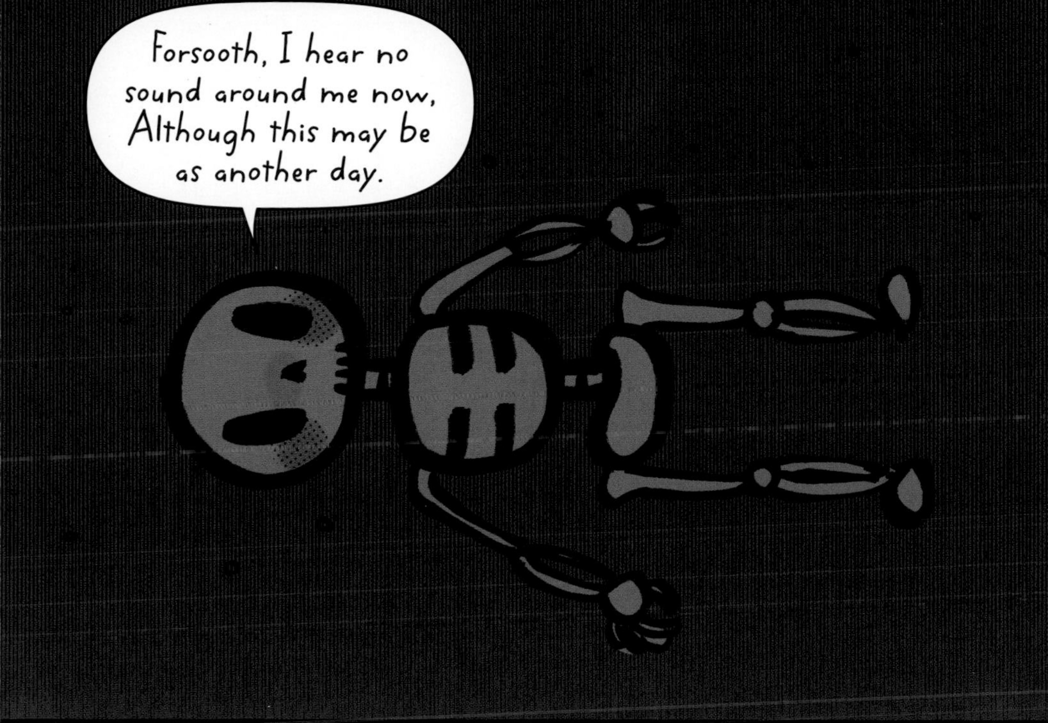
Forsooth, I hear no sound around me now, Although this may be as another day.

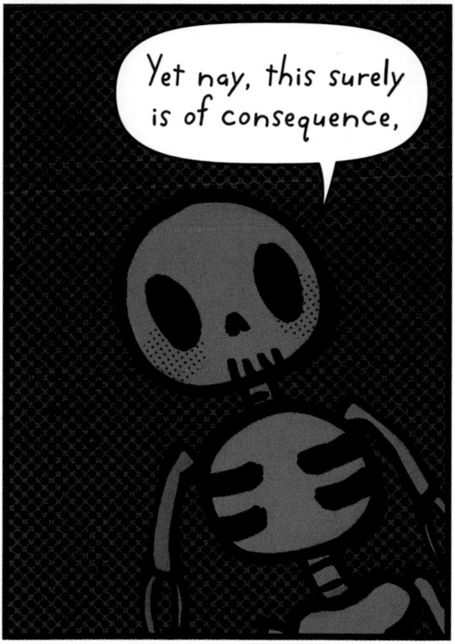
Yet nay, this surely is of consequence,

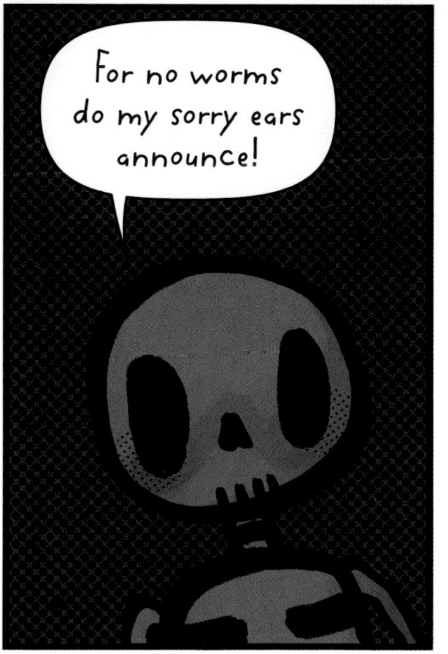
For no worms do my sorry ears announce!

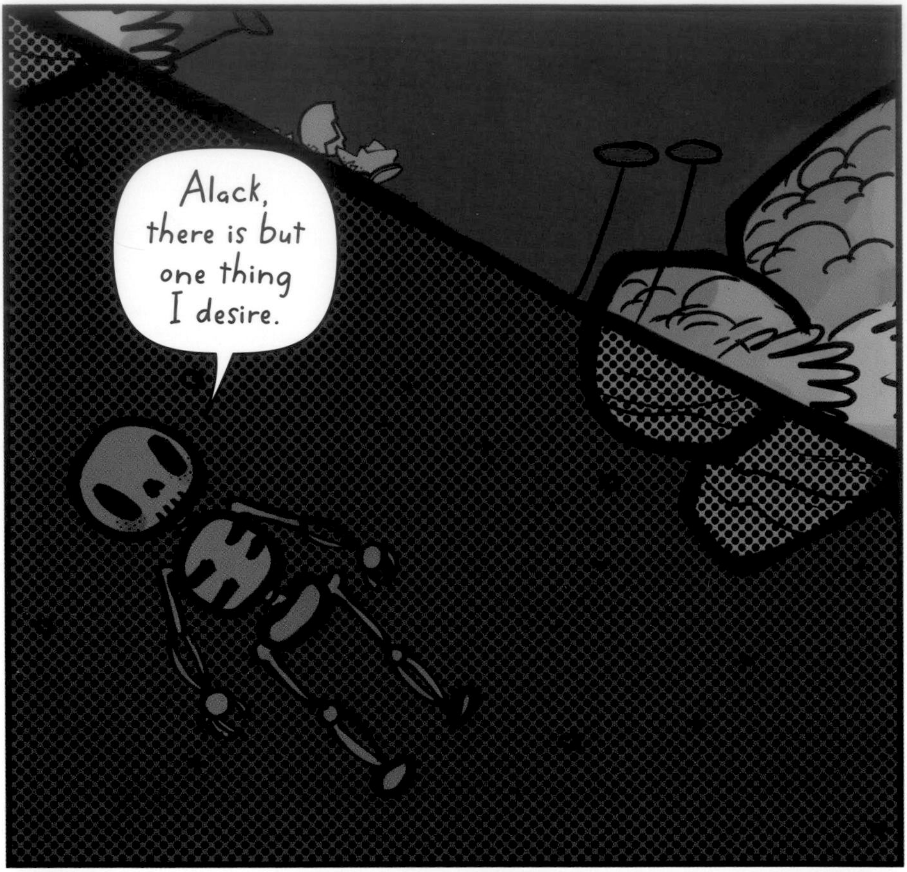
Alack, there is but one thing I desire.

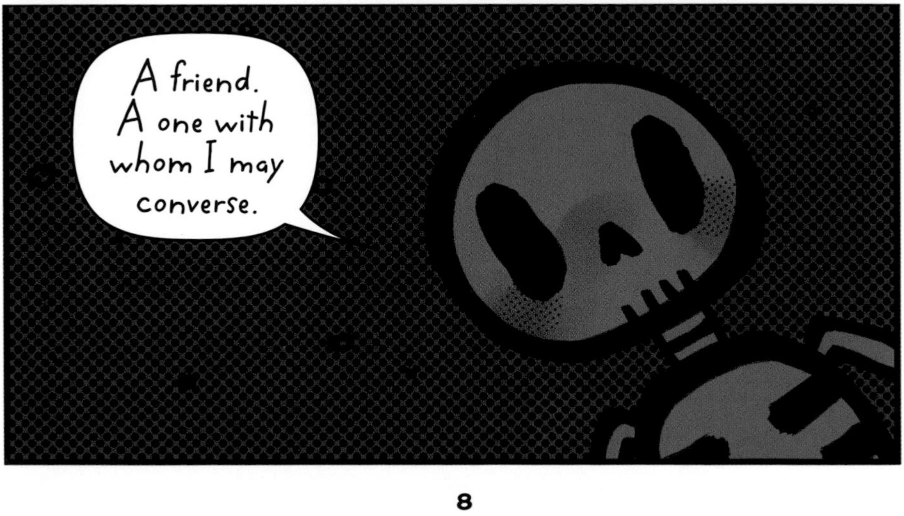
A friend. A one with whom I may converse.

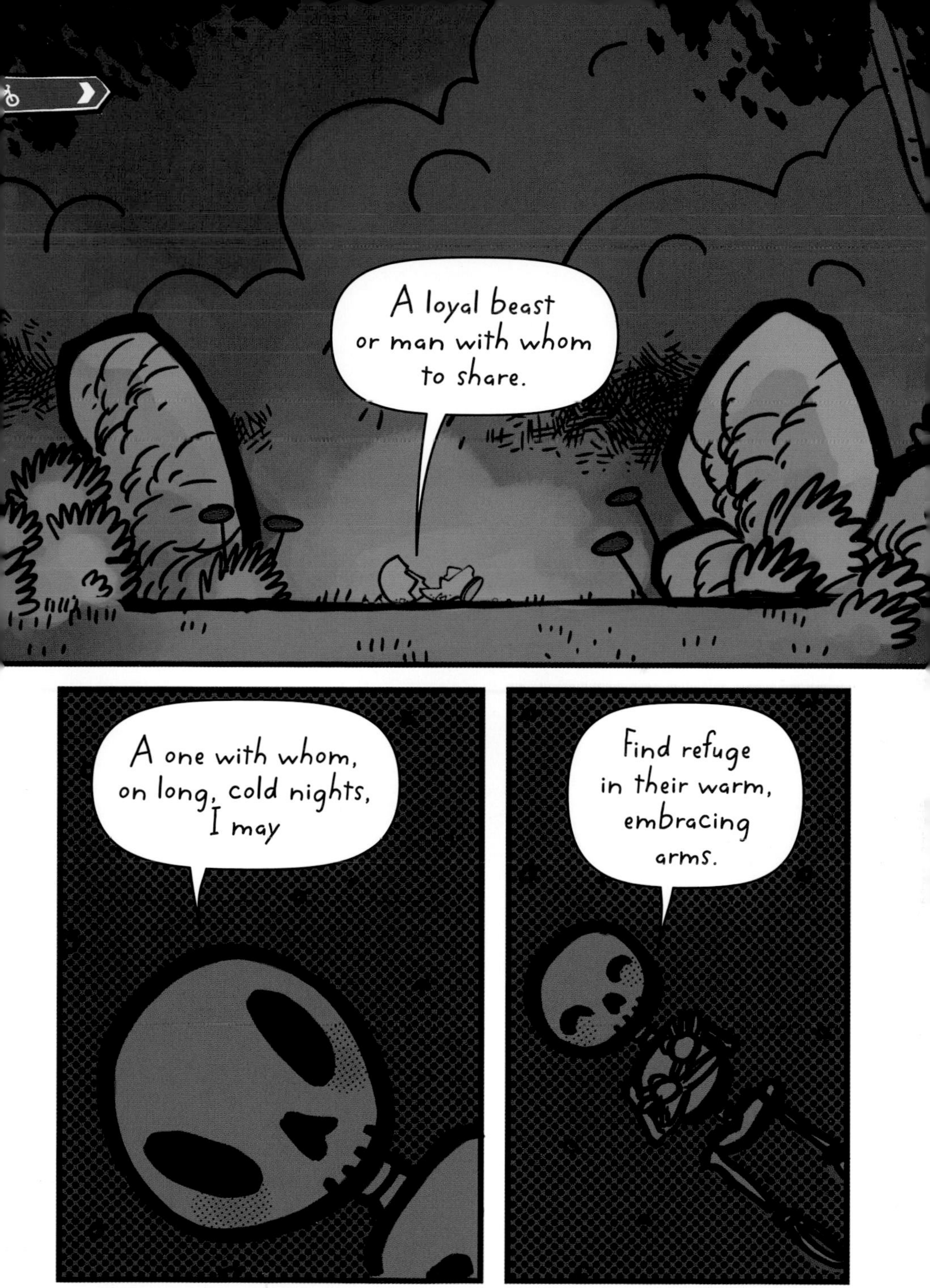
A loyal beast or man with whom to share.
A one with whom, on long, cold nights, I may
Find refuge in their warm, embracing arms.

And yet, there is another dream I wish.
A luxury beyond my mind's own lens.
A sausage would true, unreal wonder bring,
-sniff
-Sniff
If I could this and a companion take.

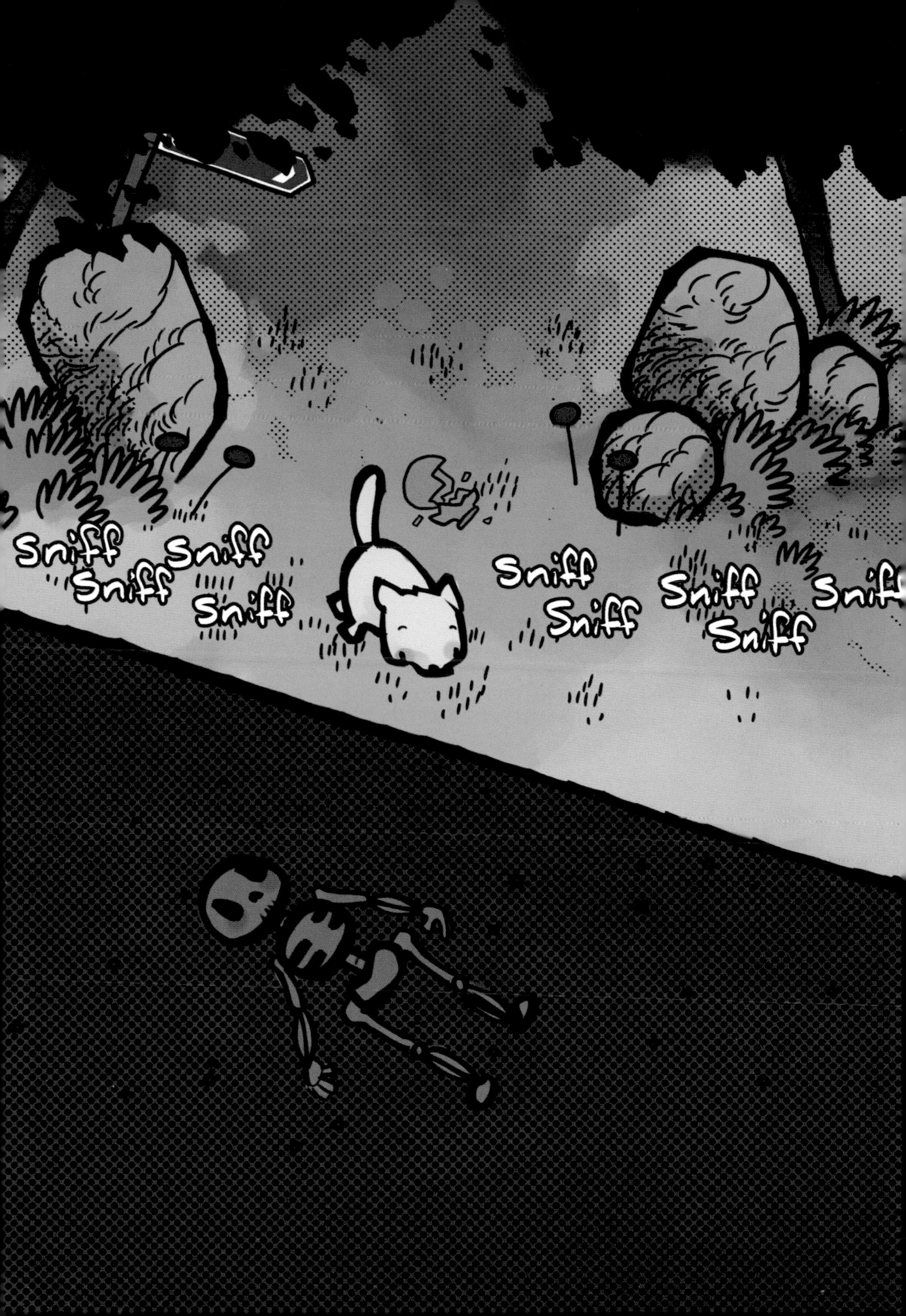
Sniff
Sniff
Sniff
Sniff
Sniff
Sniff
Sniff
Sniff
Snif

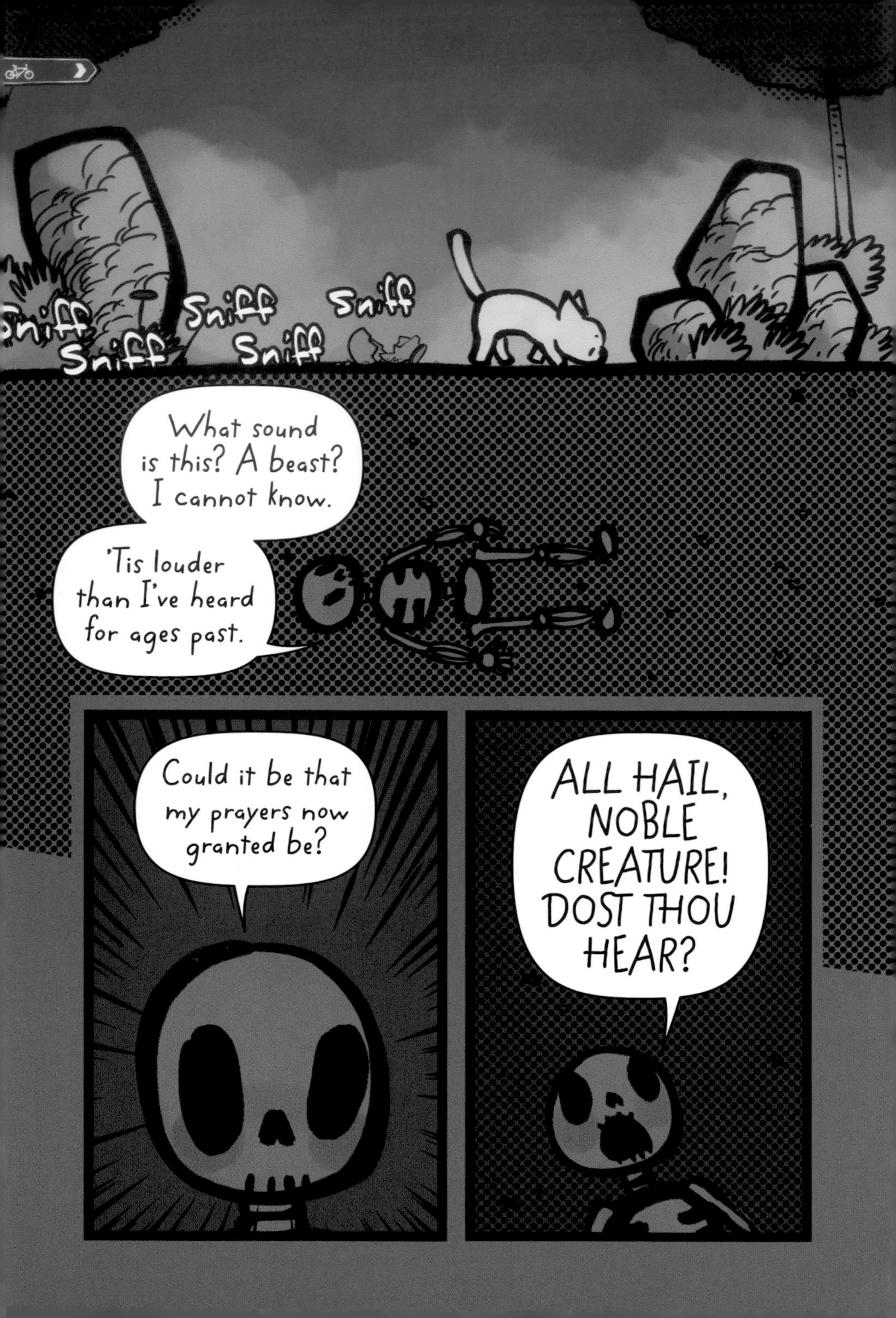

Sniff
Sniff
Sniff
Snif
Sniff
What sound is this? A beast? I cannot know.
'Tis louder than I've heard for ages past.
Could it be that my prayers now granted be?
ALL HAIL, NOBLE CREATURE! DOST THOU HEAR?

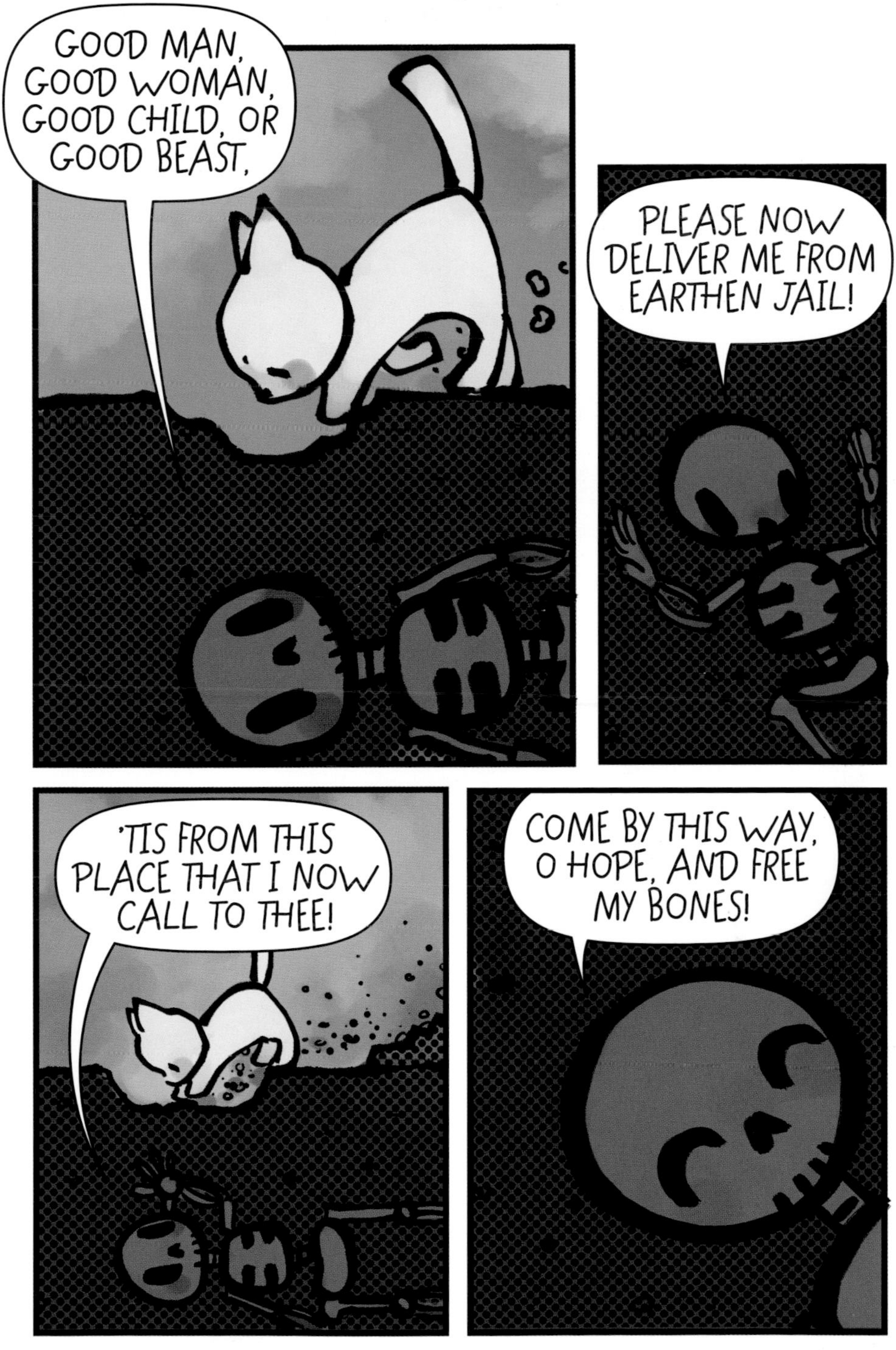
GOOD MAN, GOOD WOMAN, GOOD CHILD, OR GOOD BEAST,
PLEASE NOW DELIVER ME FROM EARTHEN JAIL!
'TIS FROM THIS PLACE THAT I NOW CALL TO THEE!
COME BY THIS WAY, O HOPE, AND FREE MY BONES!

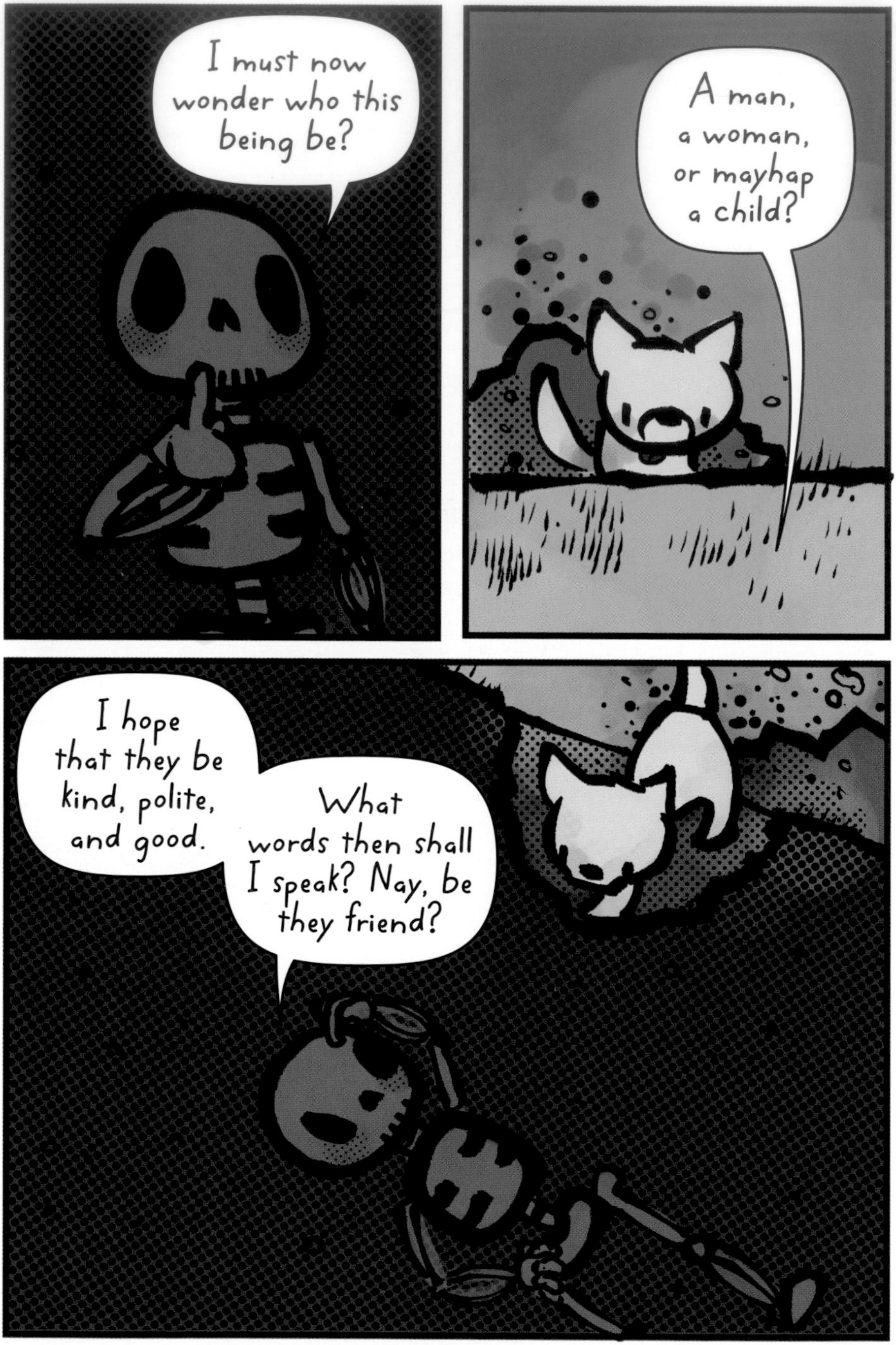
I must now wonder who this being be?
A man, a woman, or mayhap a child?
I hope that they be kind, polite, and good.
What words then shall I speak? Nay, be they friend?

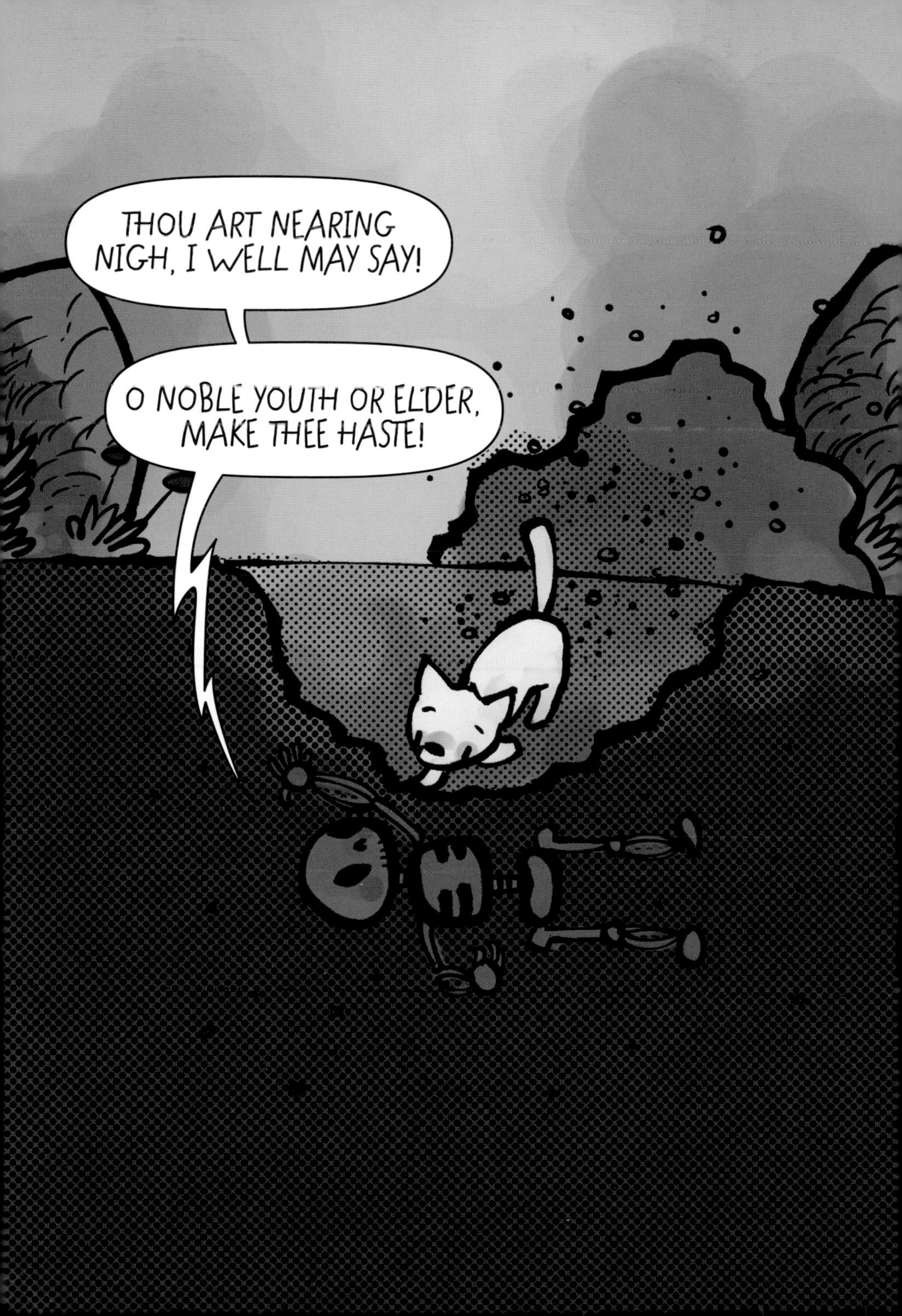
THOU ART NEARING NIGH, I WELL MAY SAY!
O NOBLE YOUTH OR ELDER, MAKE THEE HASTE!

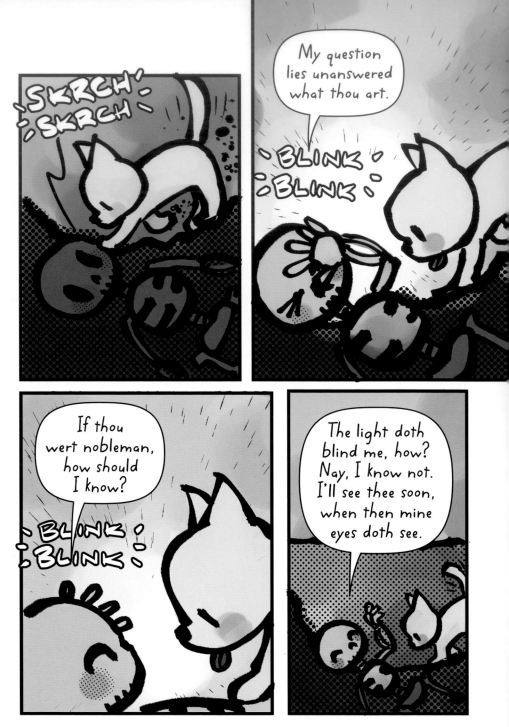

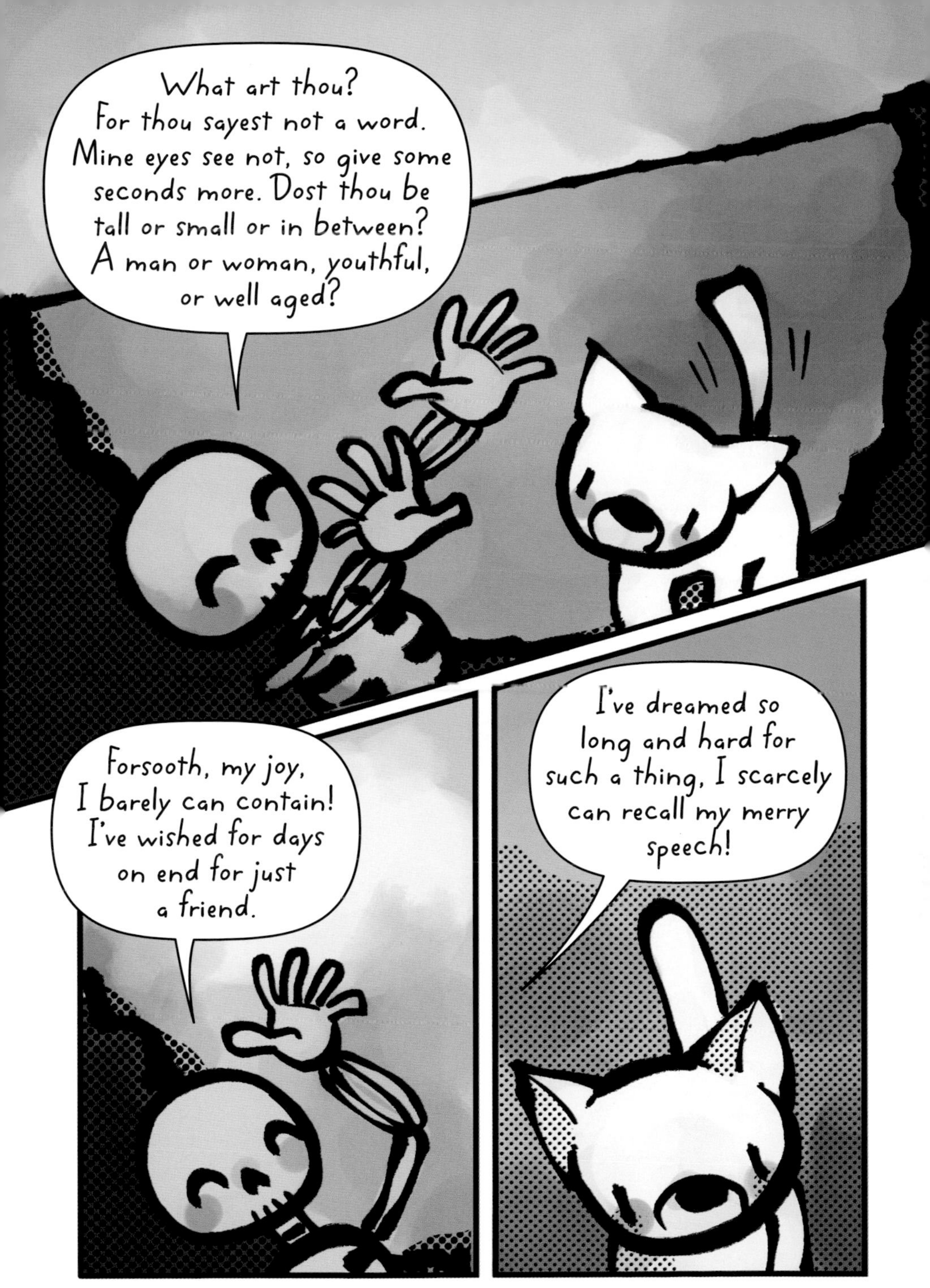
What art thou? For thou sayest not a word. Mine eyes see not, so give some seconds more. Dost thou be tall or small or in between? A man or woman, youthful, or well aged?
Forsooth, my joy, I barely can contain! I've wished for days on end for just a friend.
I've dreamed so long and hard for such a thing, I scarcely can recall my merry speech!

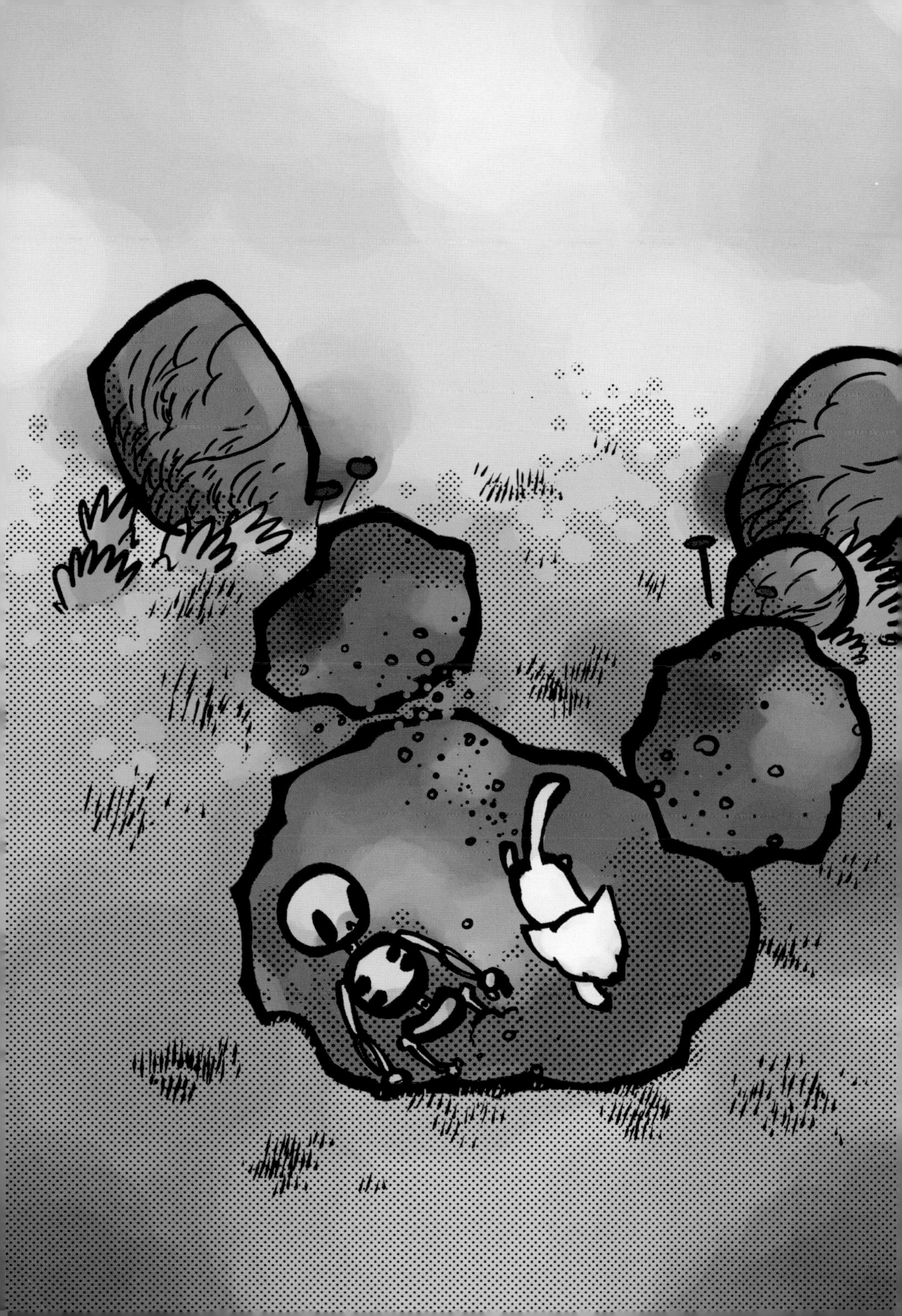

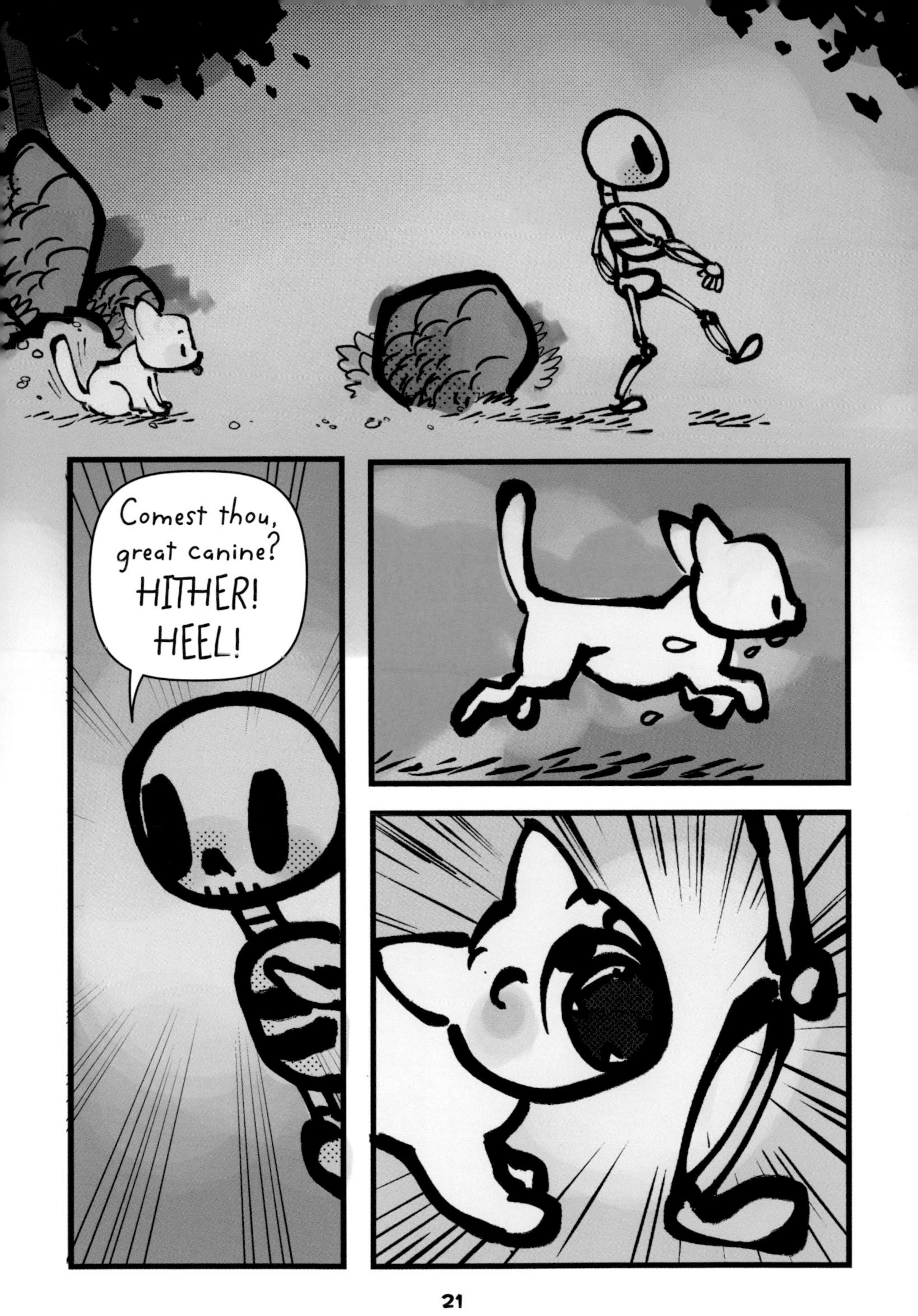
Comest thou, great canine? HITHER! HEEL!

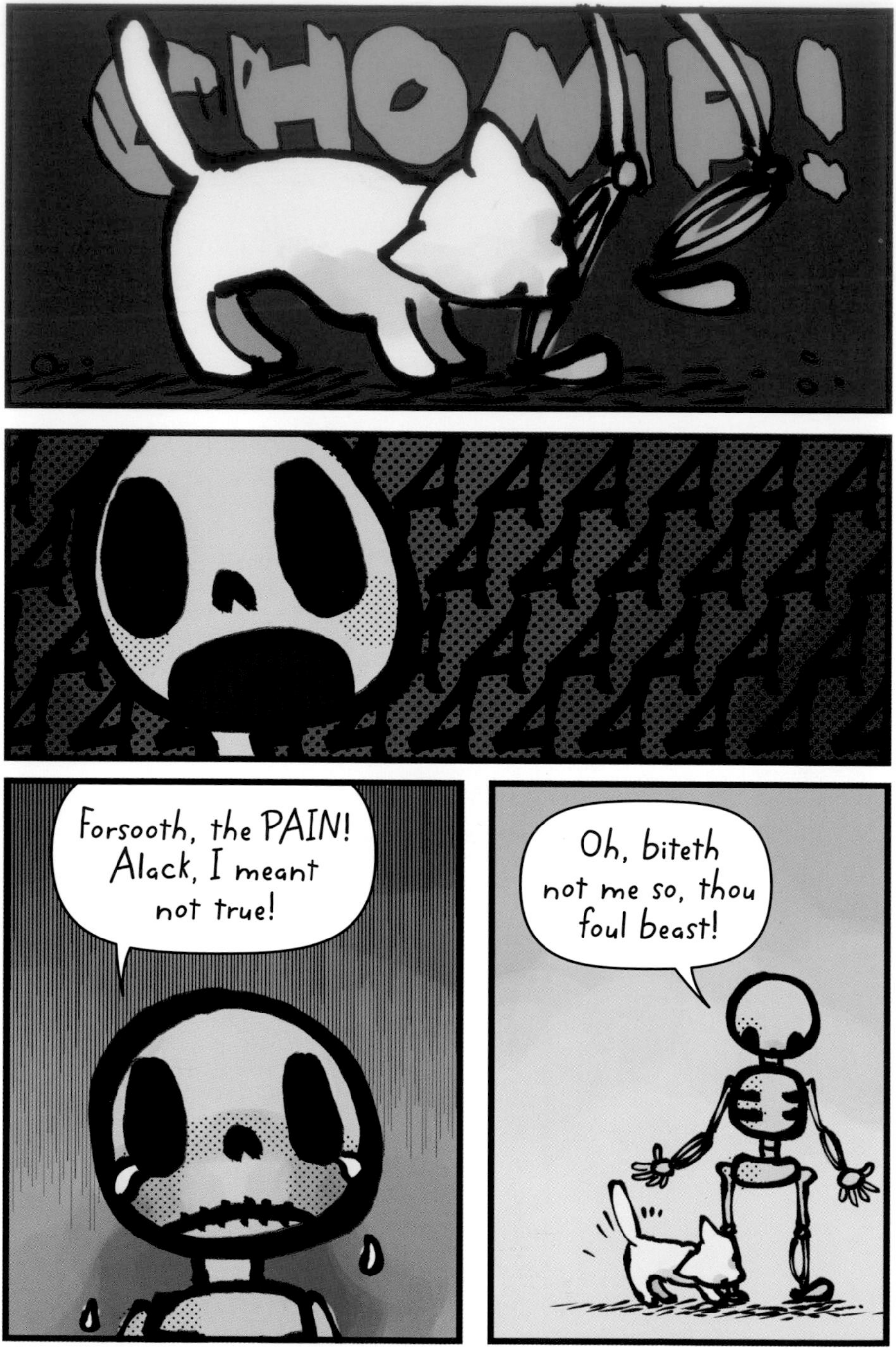

Forsooth, the PAIN! Alack, I meant not true!
Oh, biteth not me so, thou foul beast!

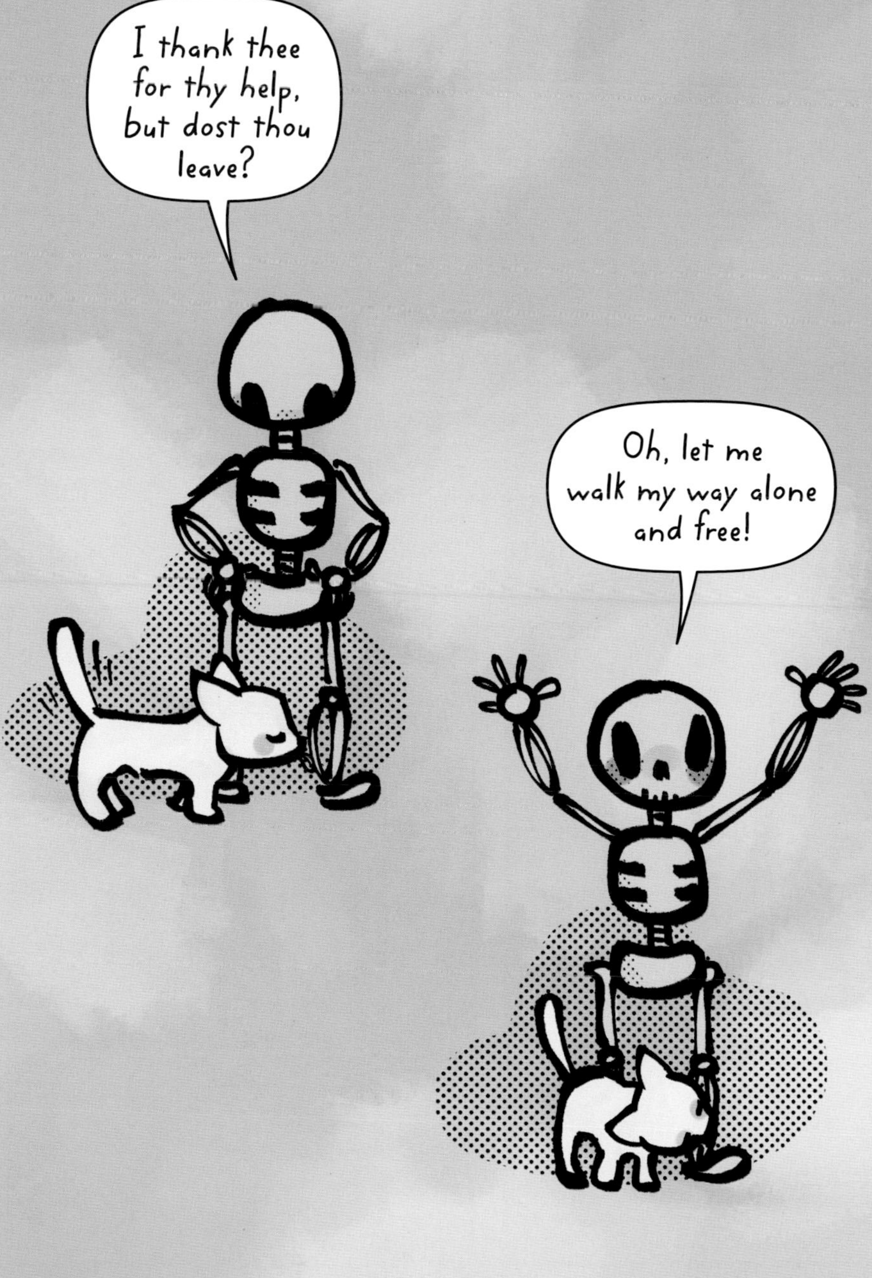
I thank thee for thy help, but dost thou leave?
Oh, let me walk my way alone and free!

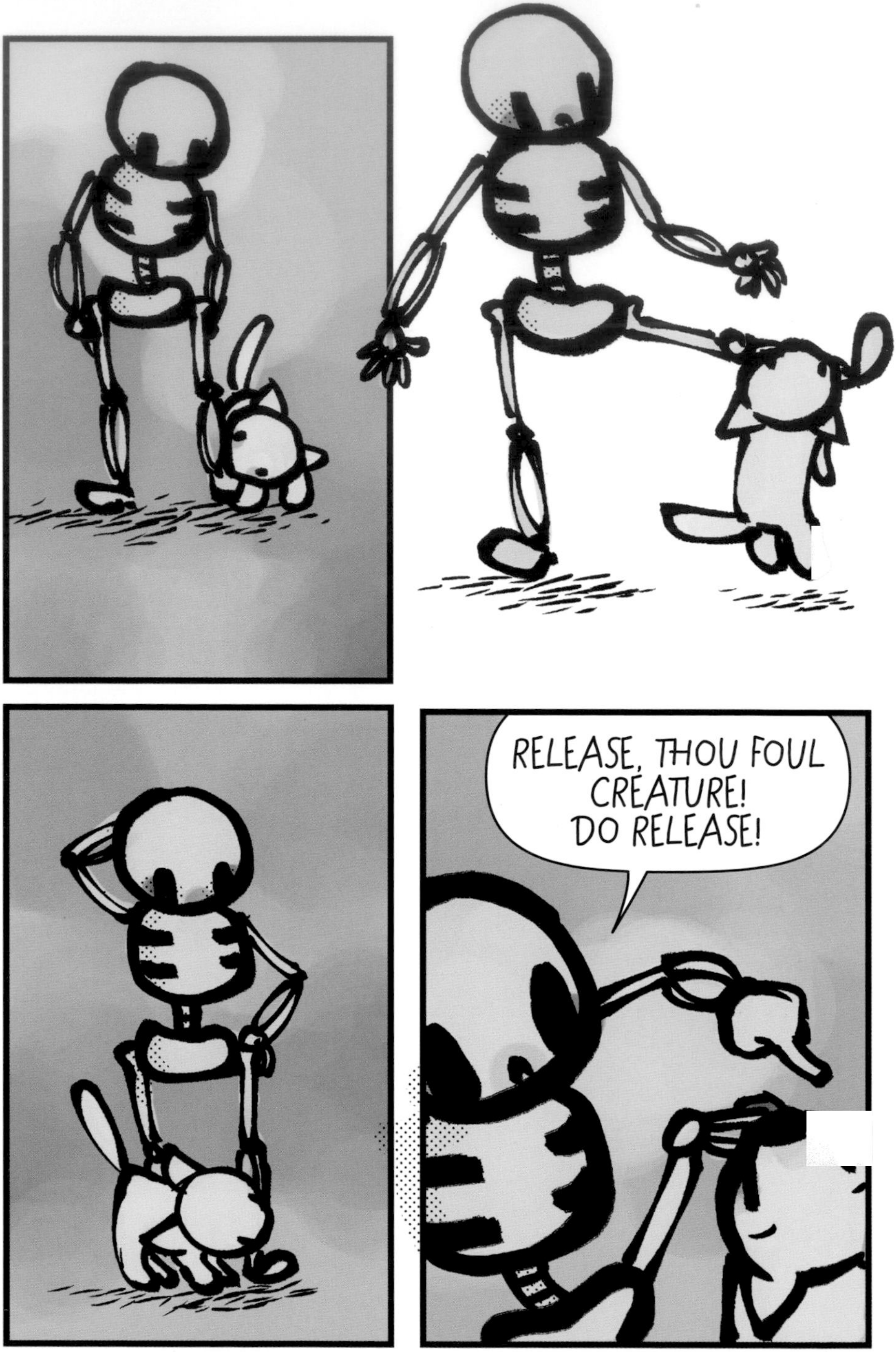
RELEASE, THOU FOUL CREATURE! DO RELEASE!

26

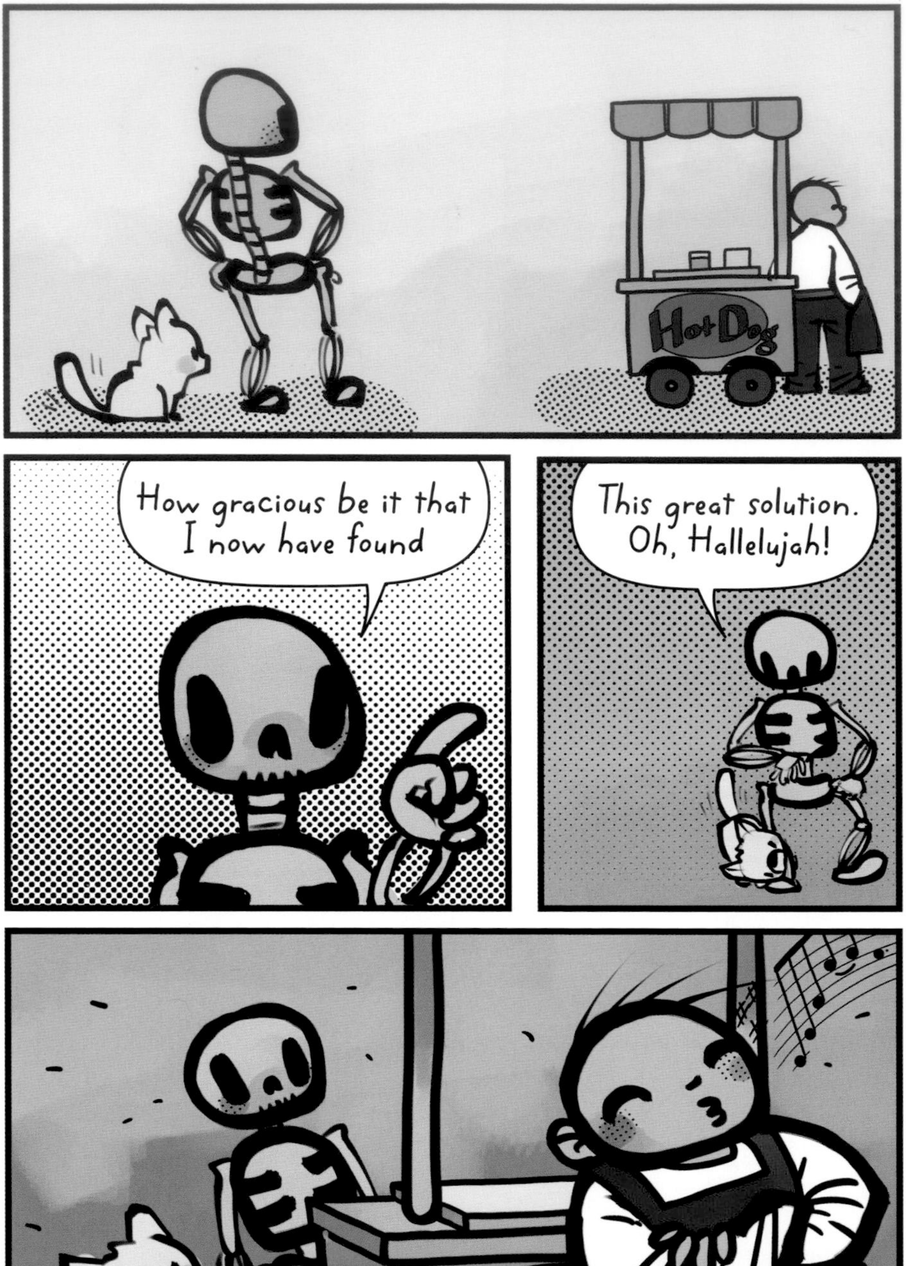
Hot Dog
How gracious be it that I now have found
This great solution. Oh, Hallelujah!

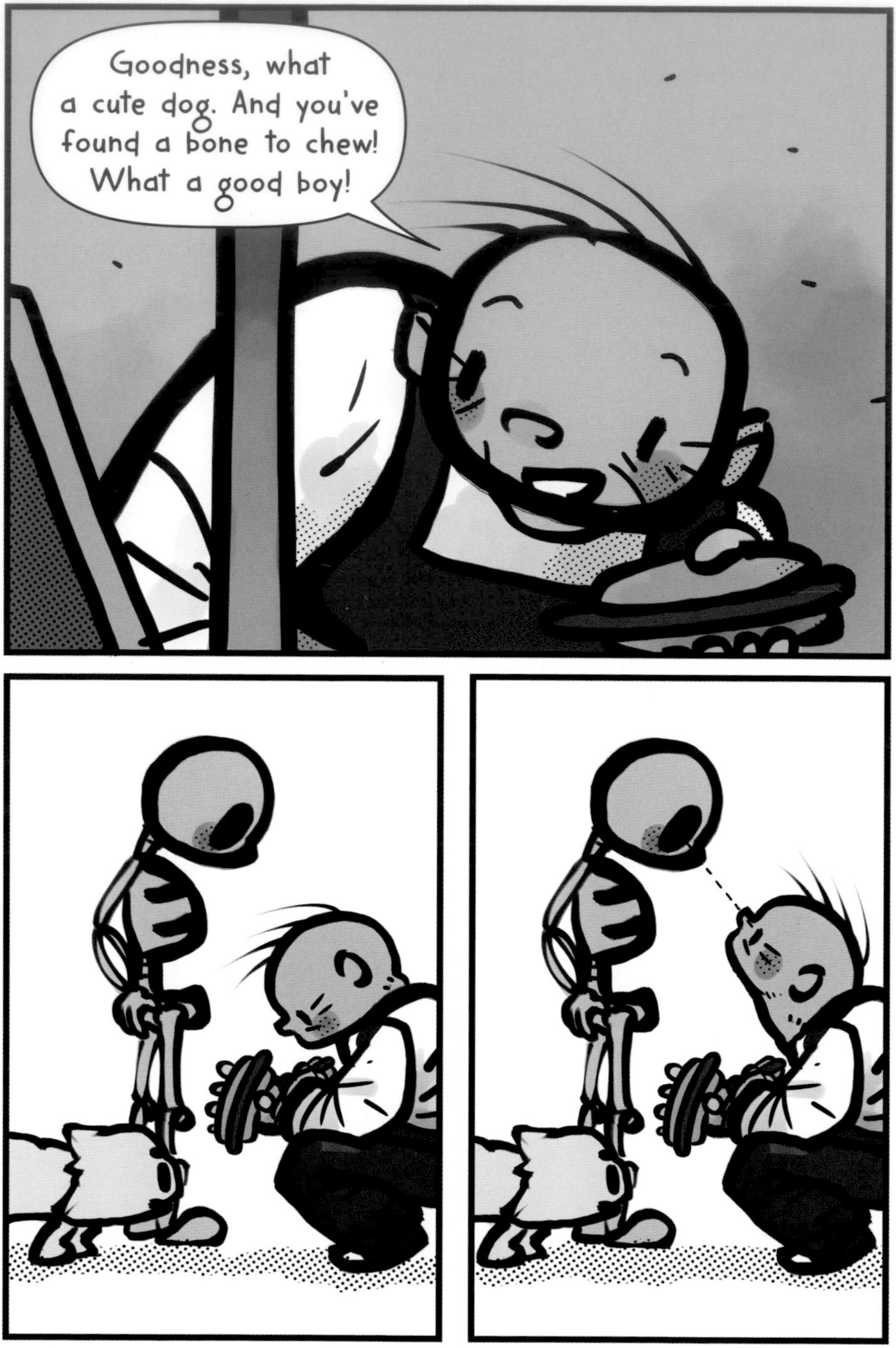
Goodness, what a cute dog. And you've found a bone to chew! What a good boy!

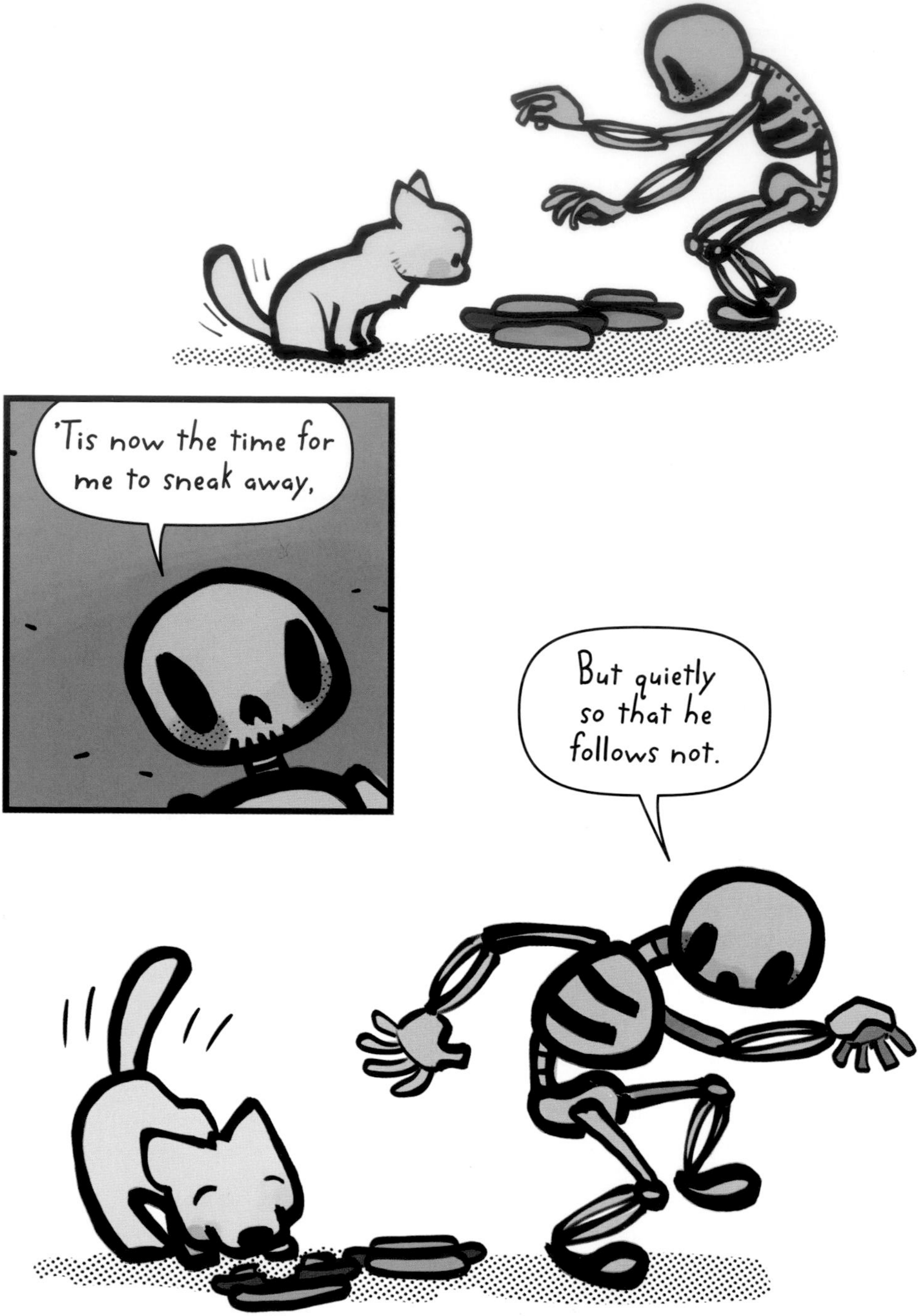
'Tis now the time for me to sneak away,
But quietly so that he follows not.

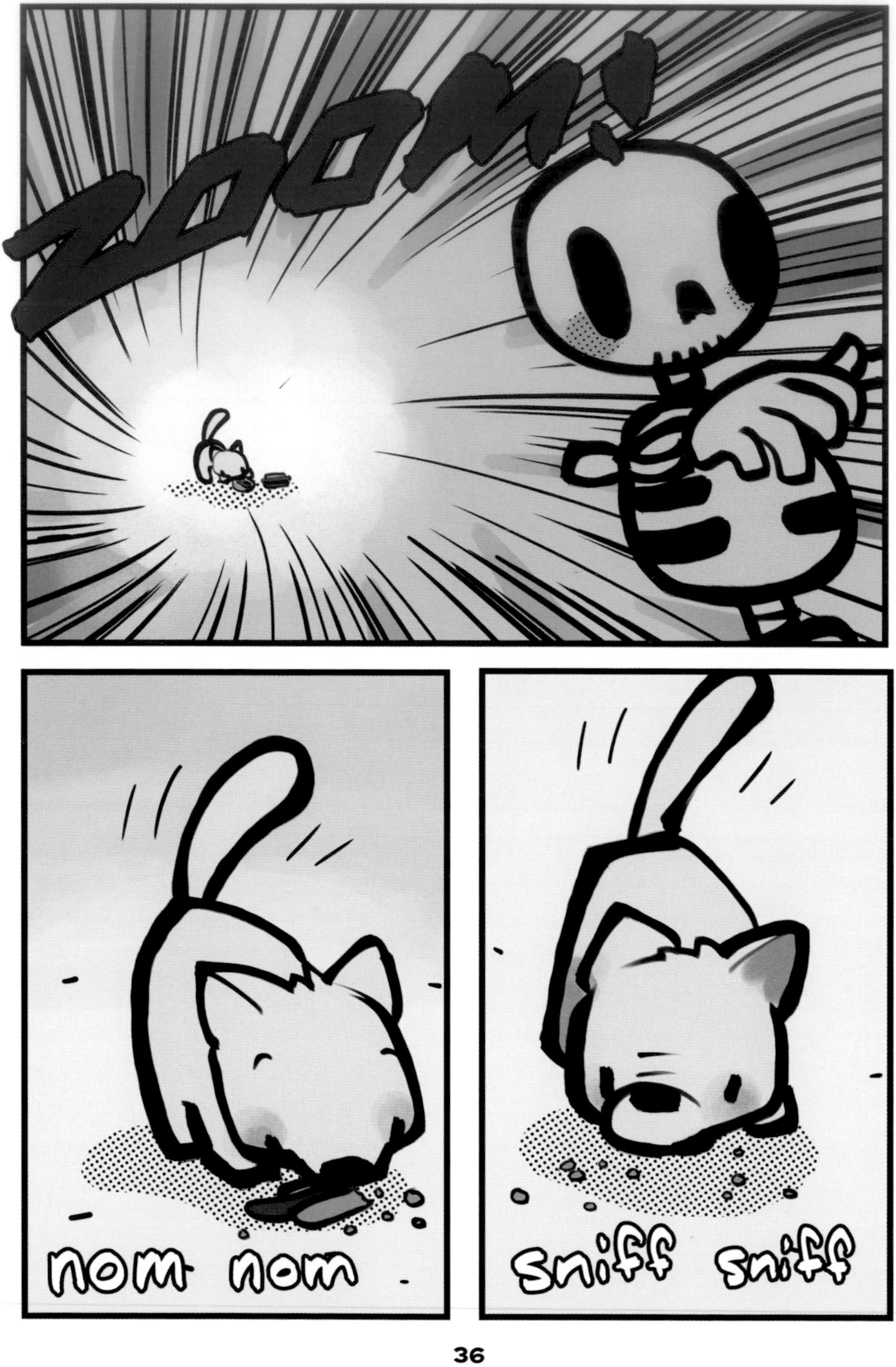
ZOOM!
nom nom
sniff sniff

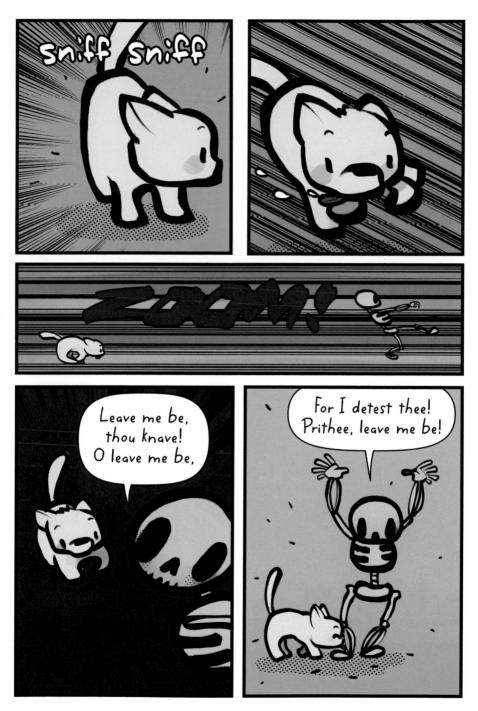

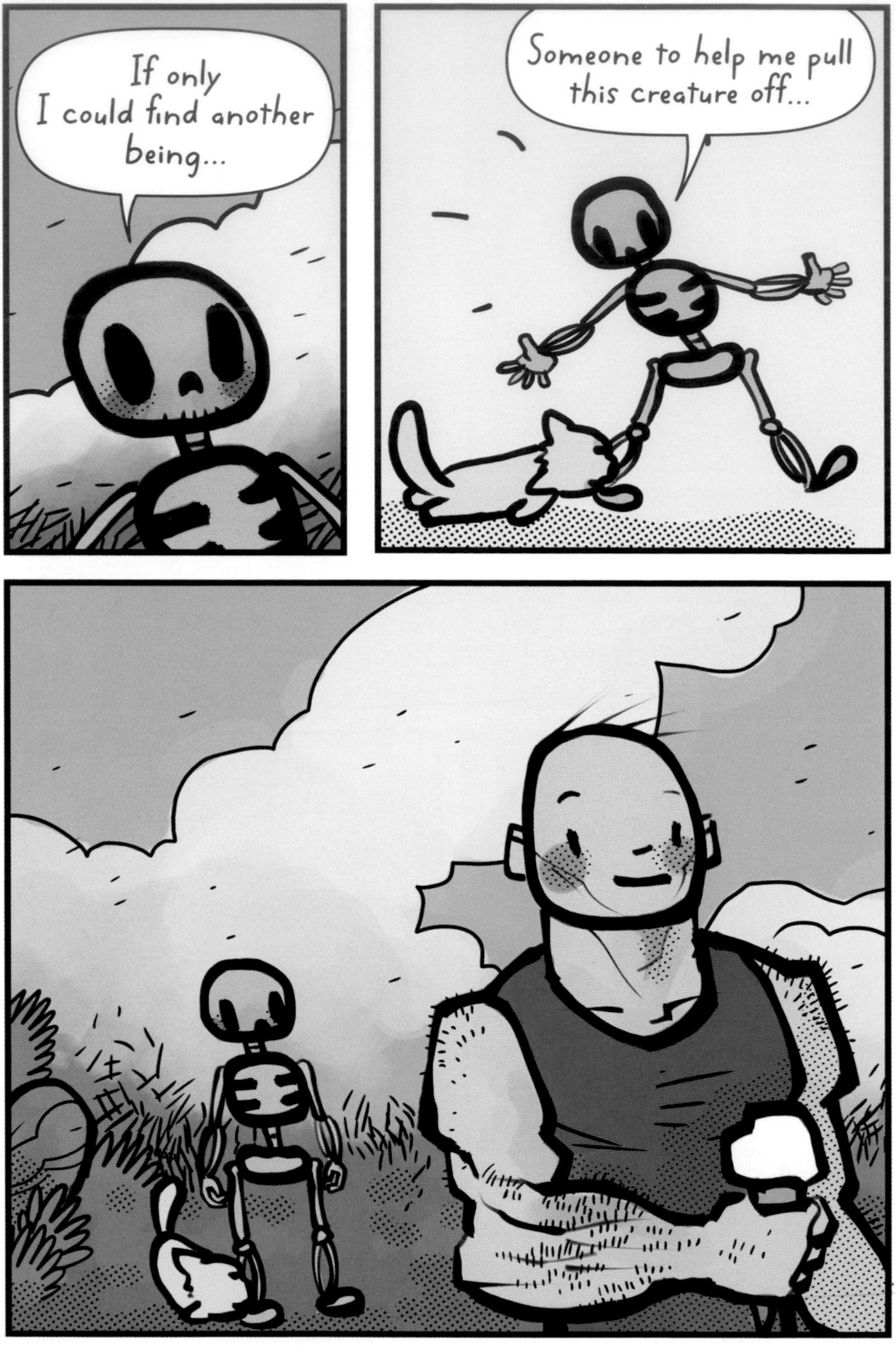
If only I could find another being...
Someone to help me pull this creature off...

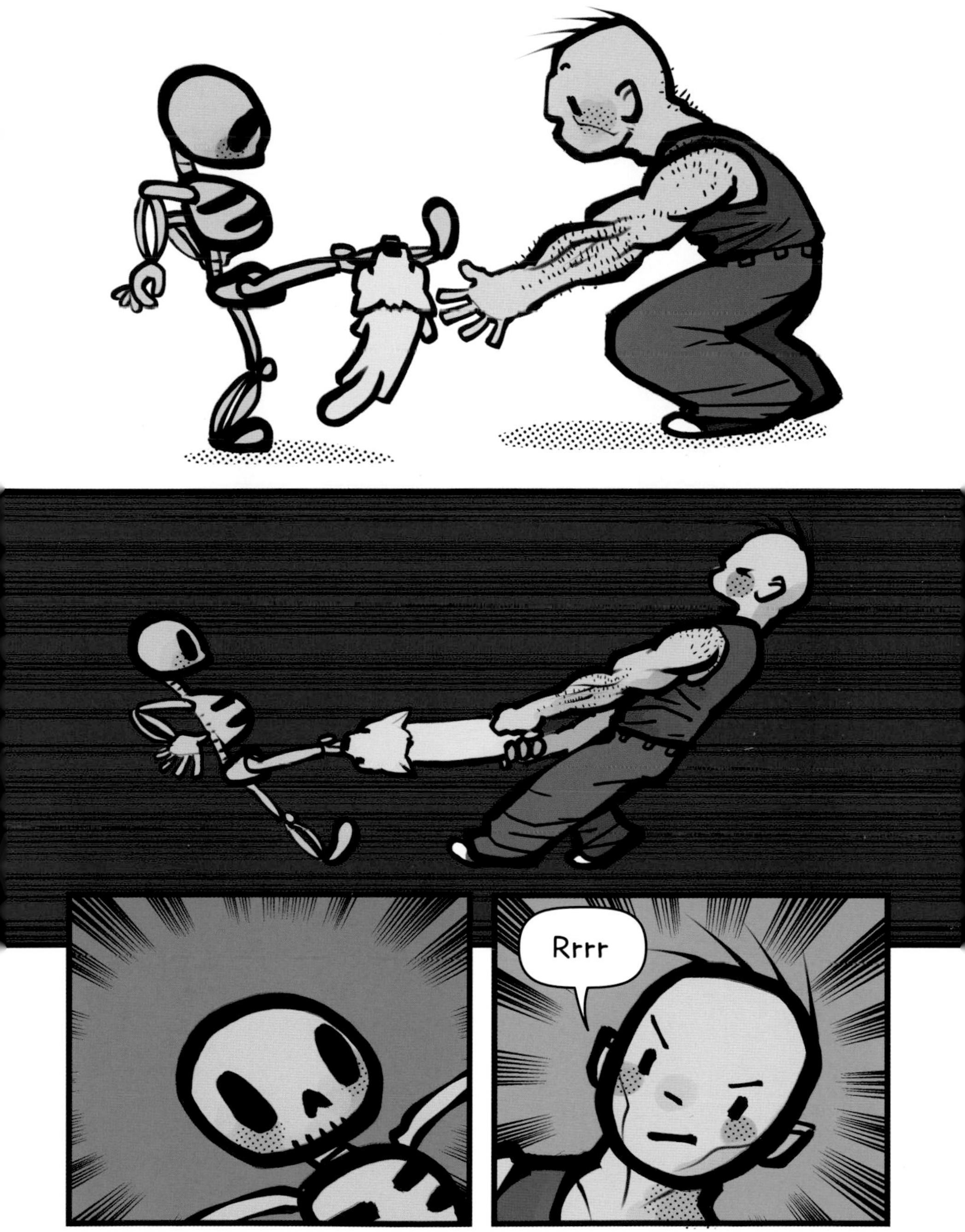
Rrrr

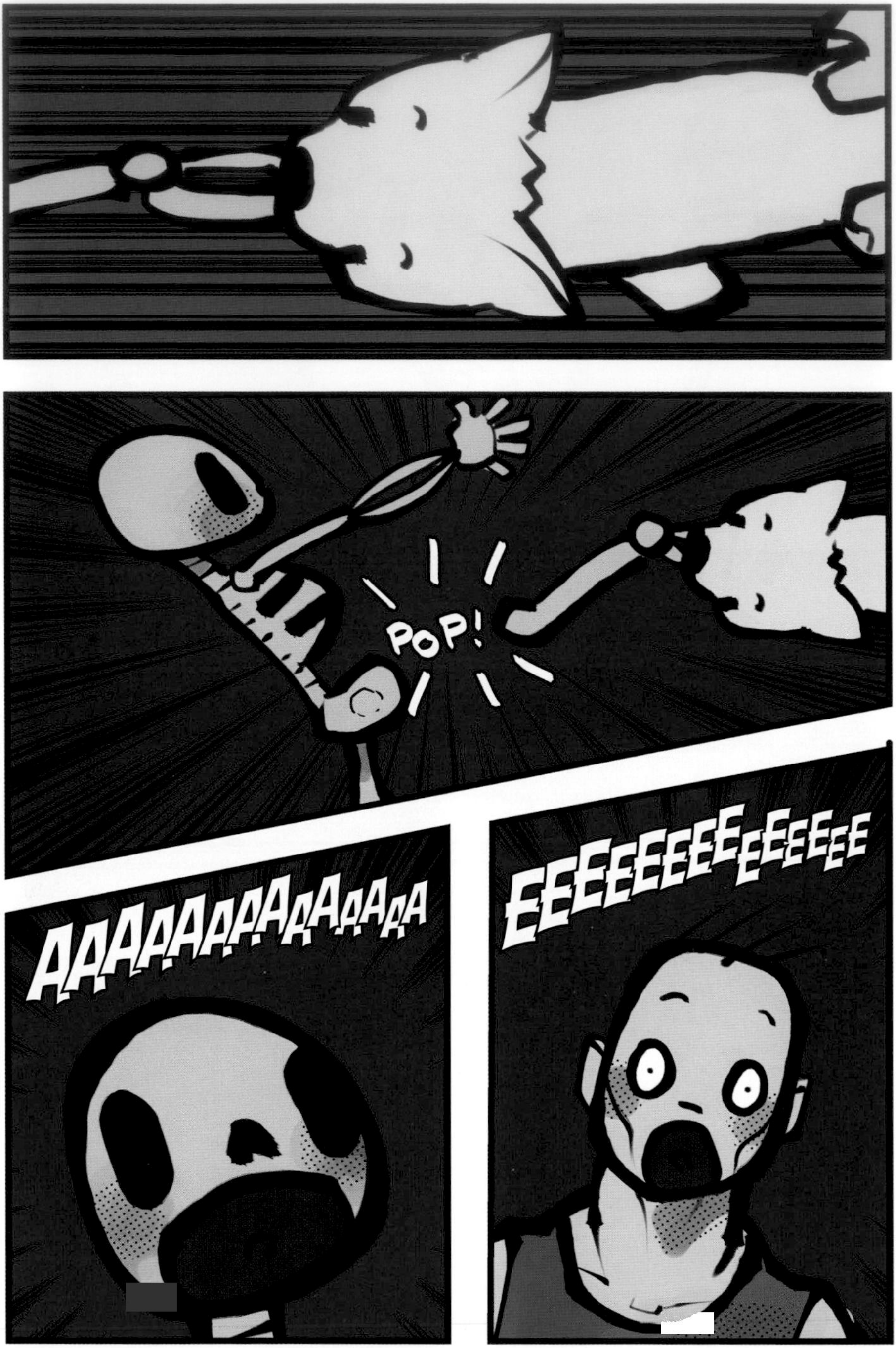
POP!
AAAAAAAAAAAA
EEEEEEEEEEEEEEE

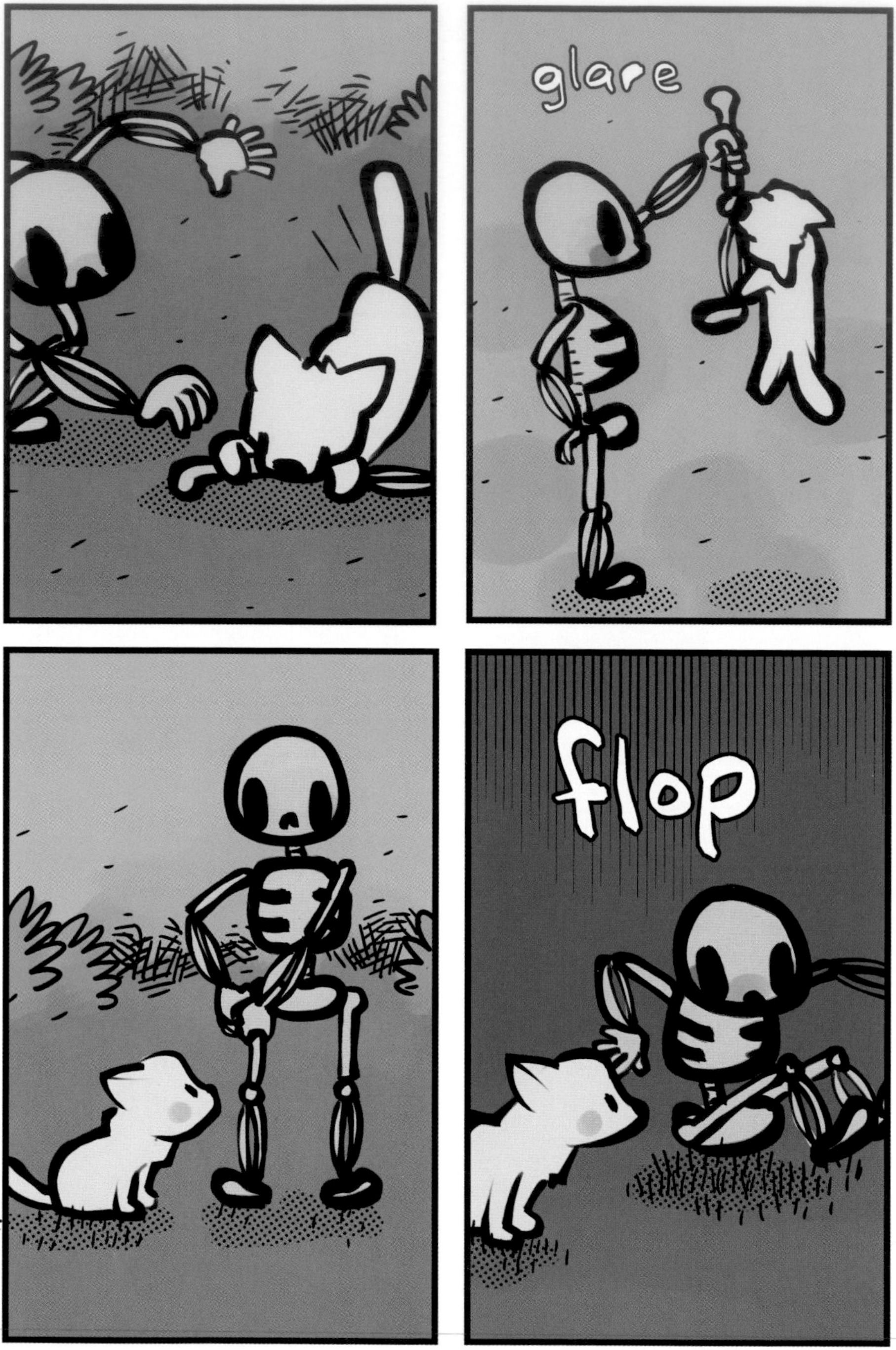
glare
flop

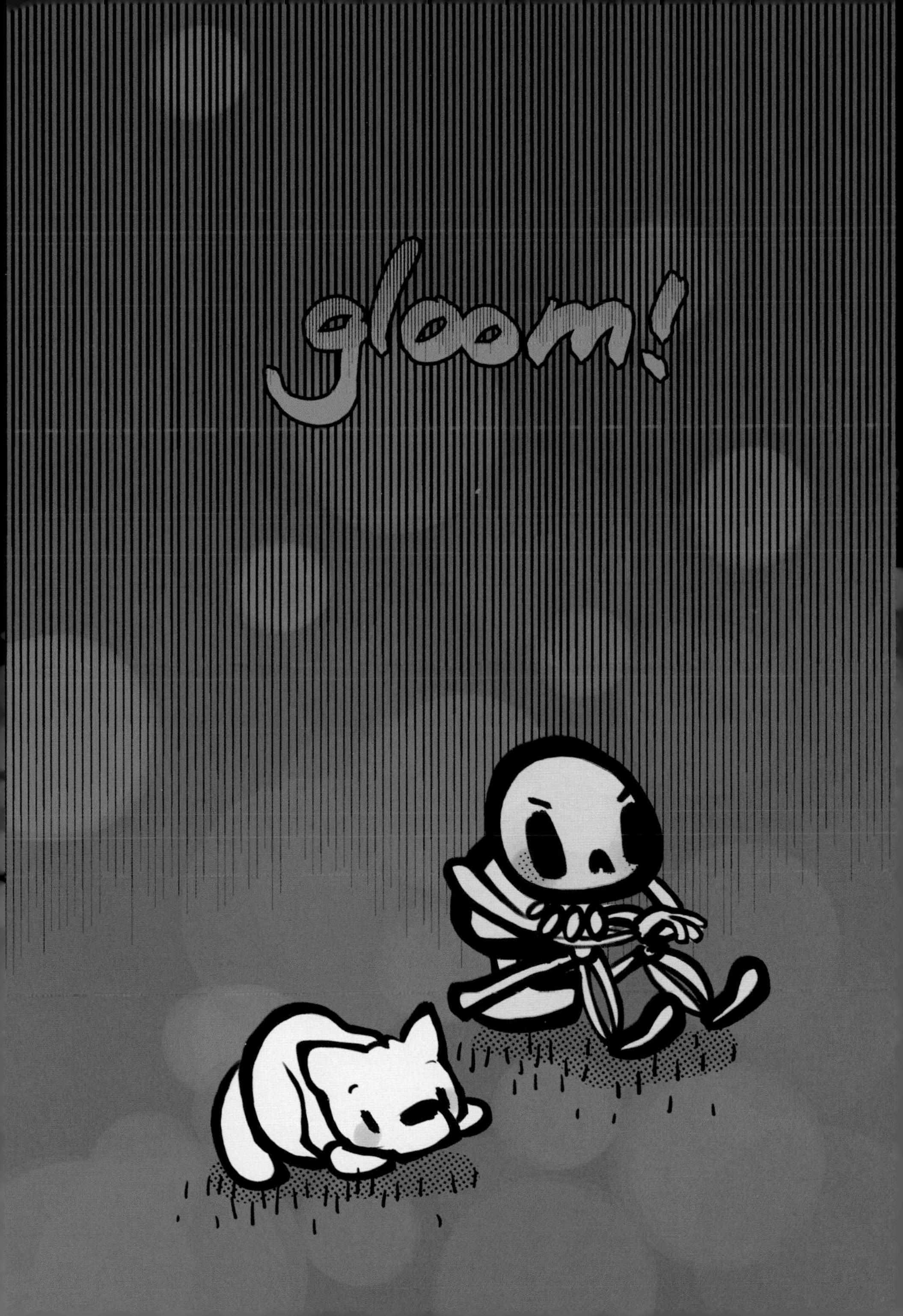
gloom!

ACT TWO:

MAN'S PEST FRIEND

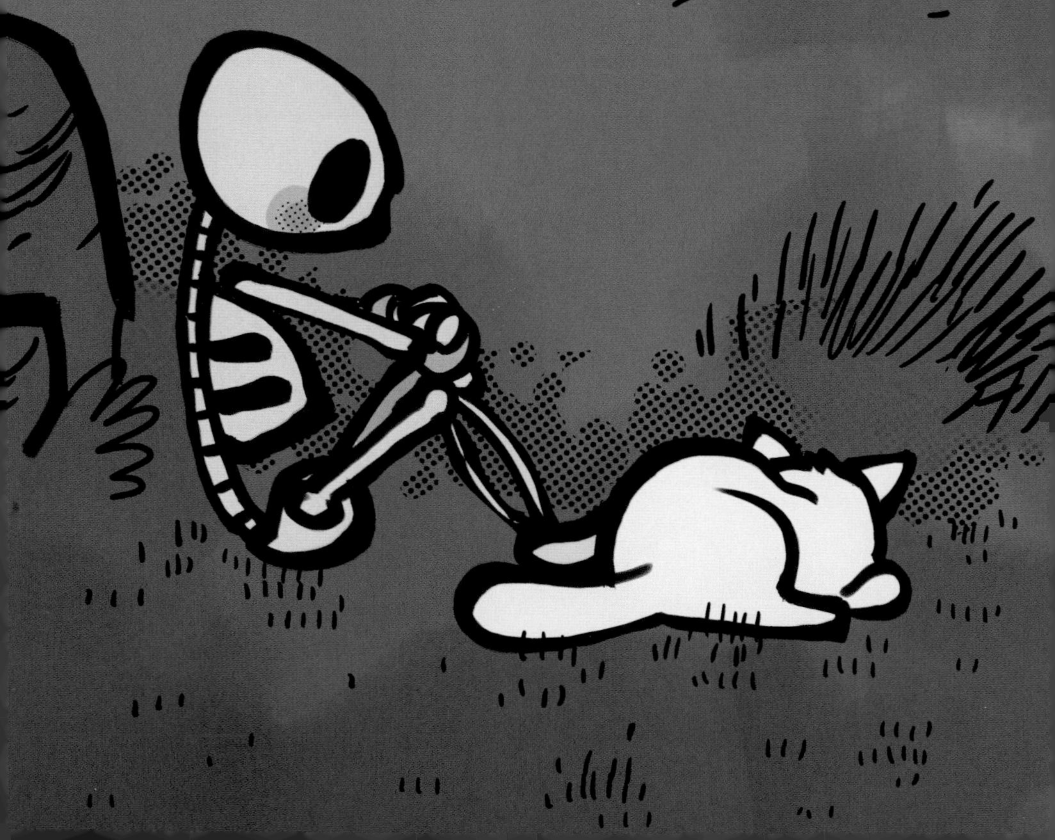

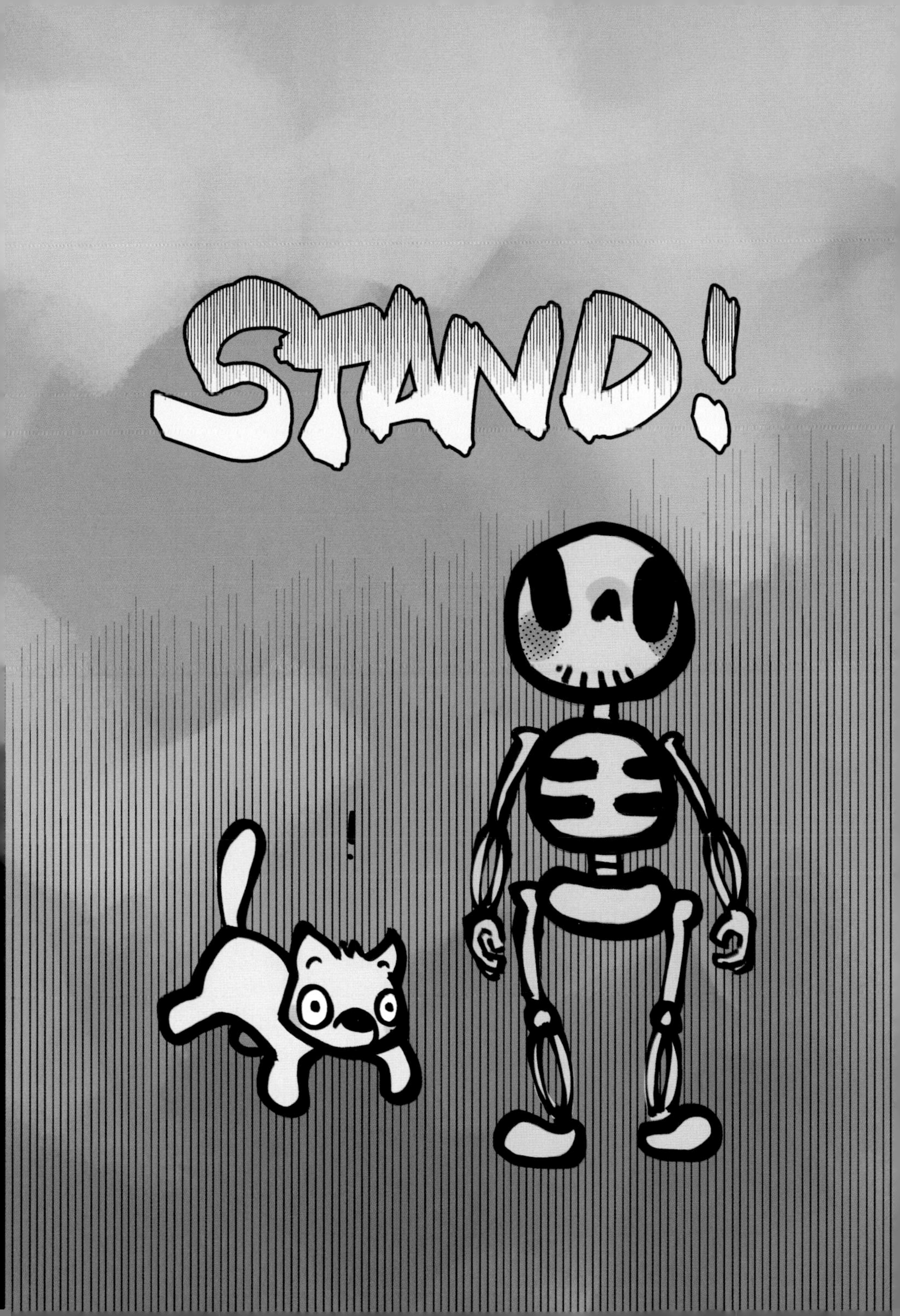
STAND!
!

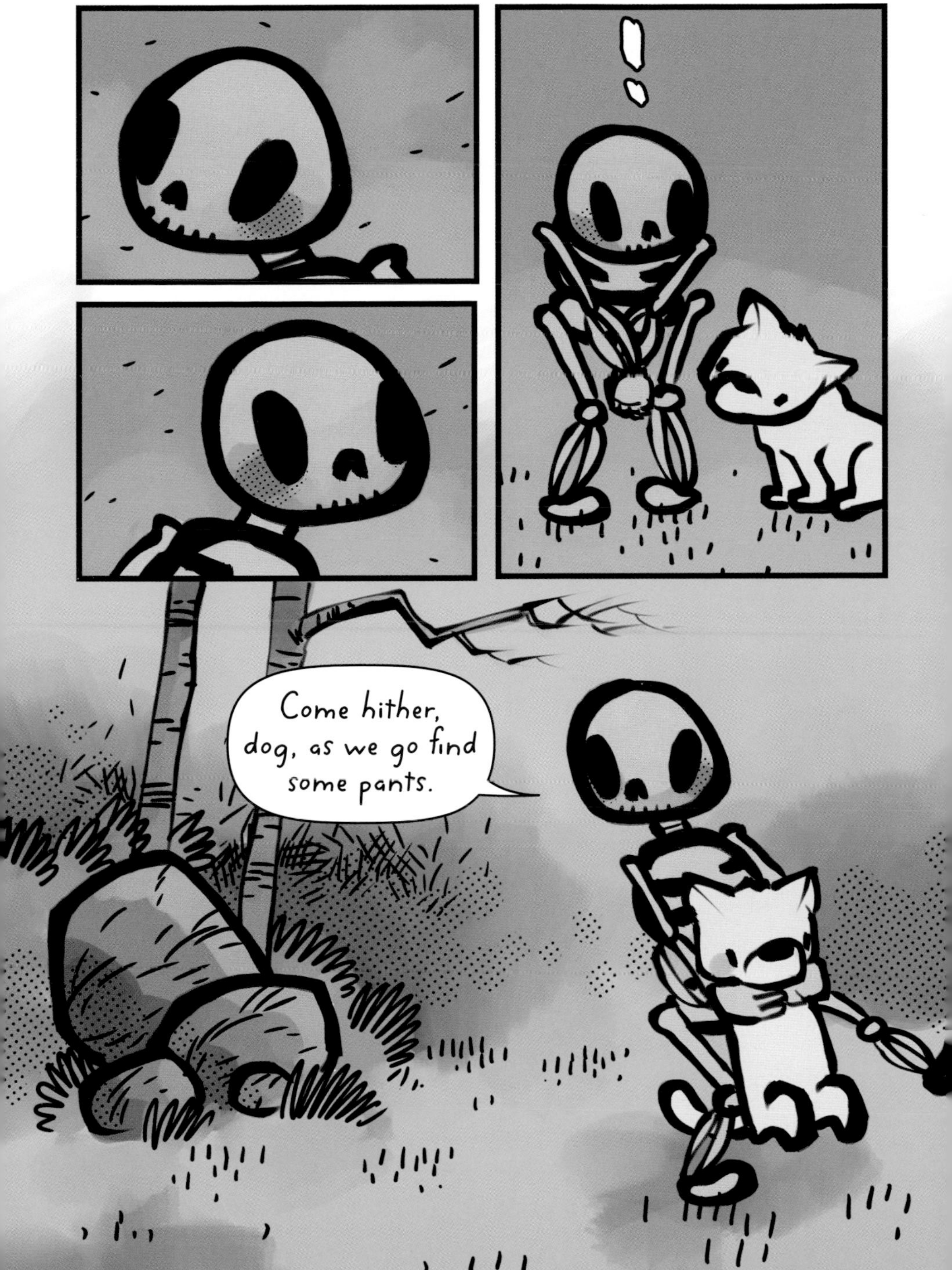
!
Come hither, dog, as we go find some pants.

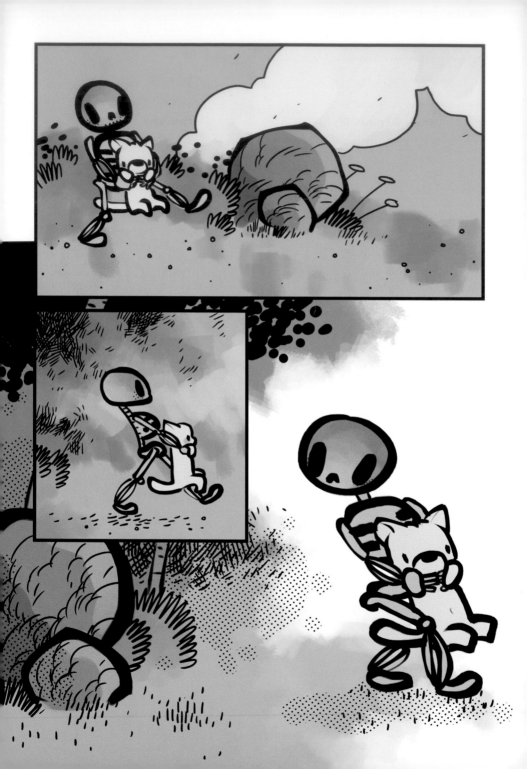

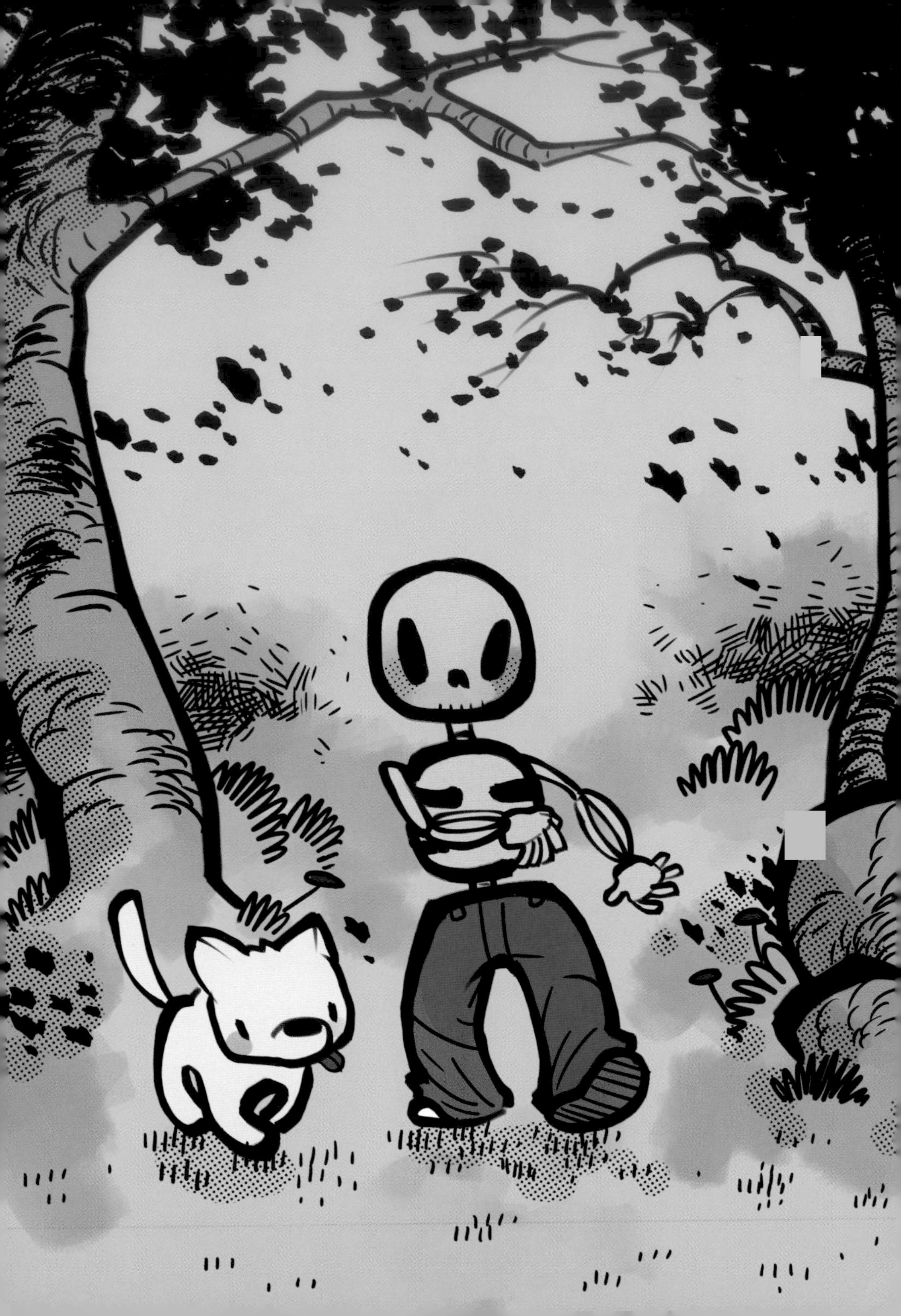

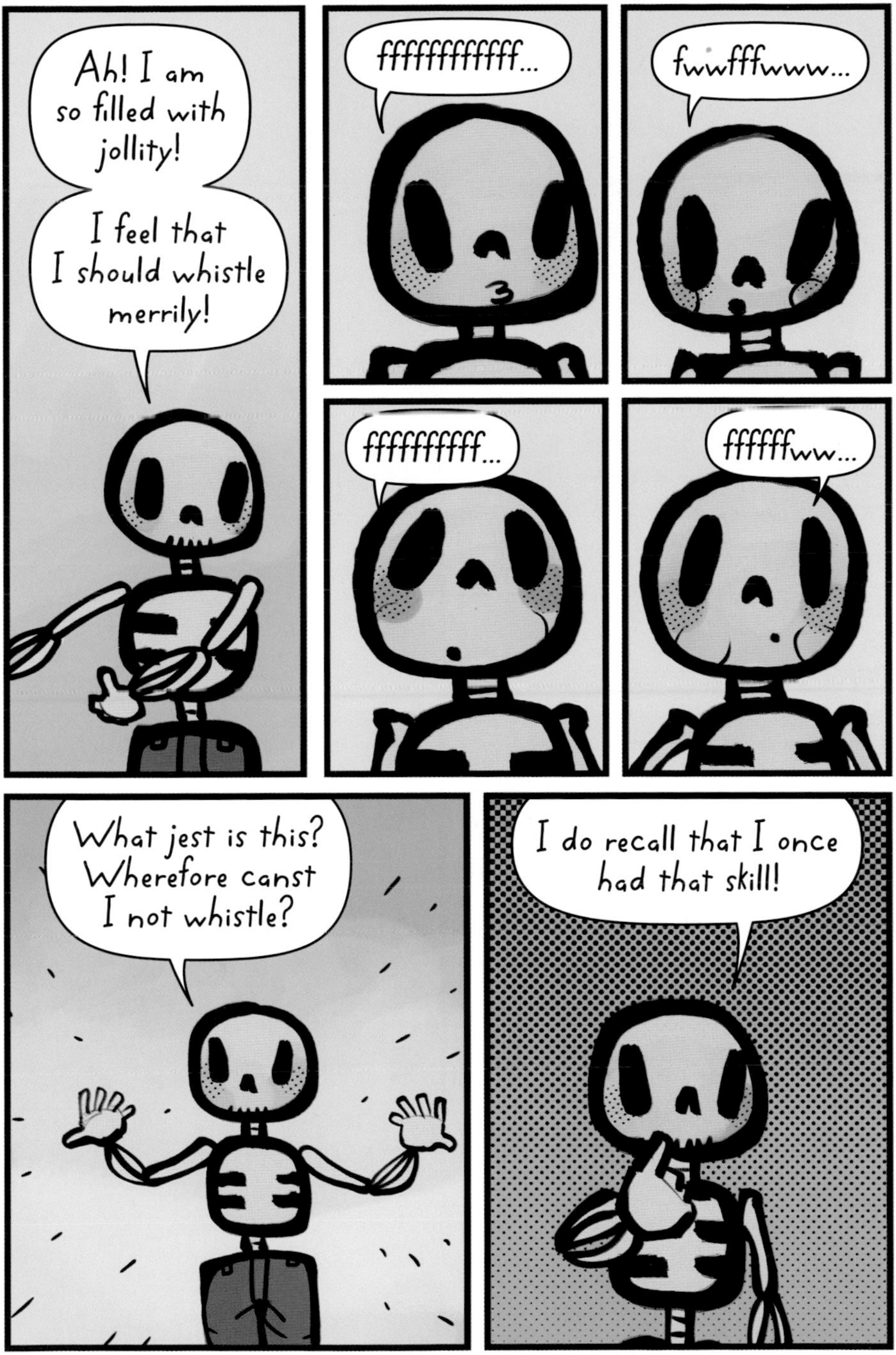
Ah! I am so filled with jollity!
I feel that I should whistle merrily!
ffffffffffff...
fwwfffwww...
ffffffffff...
ffffffww...
What jest is this? Wherefore canst I not whistle?
I do recall that I once had that skill!

Pray, get thee unto him! I wish thee luck!
BARK! BARK! YAP! BARK!
BARK! YAP!
Oh, hello! Where did you come from?
LICK
Ha ha ha! Gross! Ha ha!

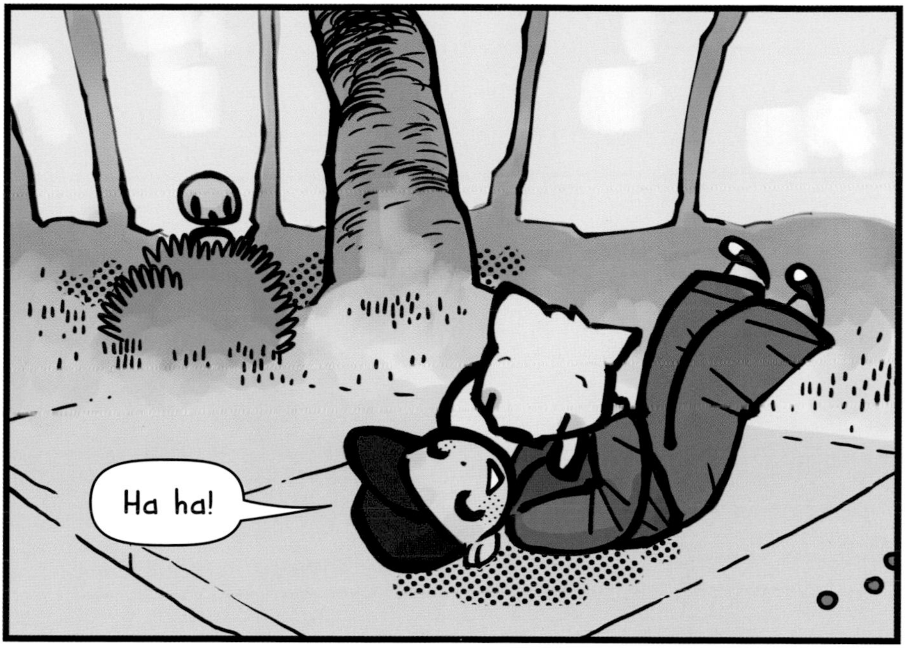
Ha ha!

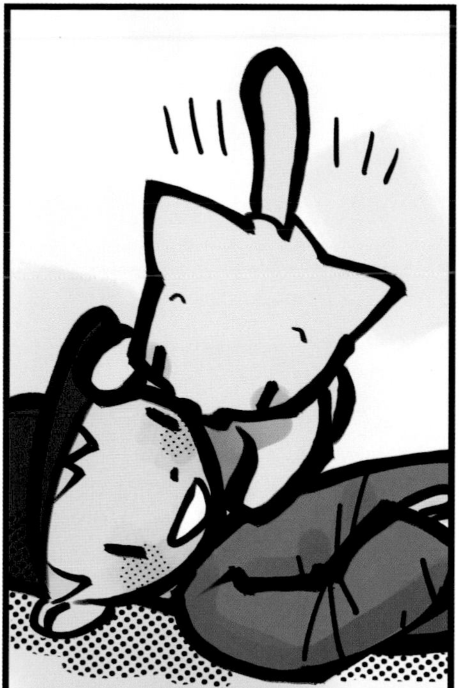

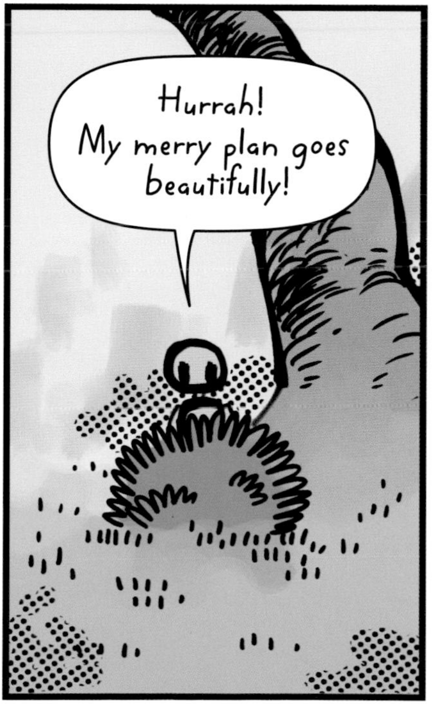
Hurrah!
My merry plan goes beautifully!

I do recall that in those days of old,
I was among the best of marble players.
Indeed, I was quite famous for that skill!
And so, this boy and I shall be good friends.

Mayhap, when we have tired of marble-rolling,
We'll play at hopscotch or at archery?
I wonder if his skills can measure mine?

71

O, thank the heavens! We have got away!
PANT PANT!
PANT PANT PANT
I hope that poor young boy is safely hid.
It would be worse indeed if such events shone all their dark fear on us again.
A skeleton is not a joyful thing, And I'll admit, it makes me quite afear'd.

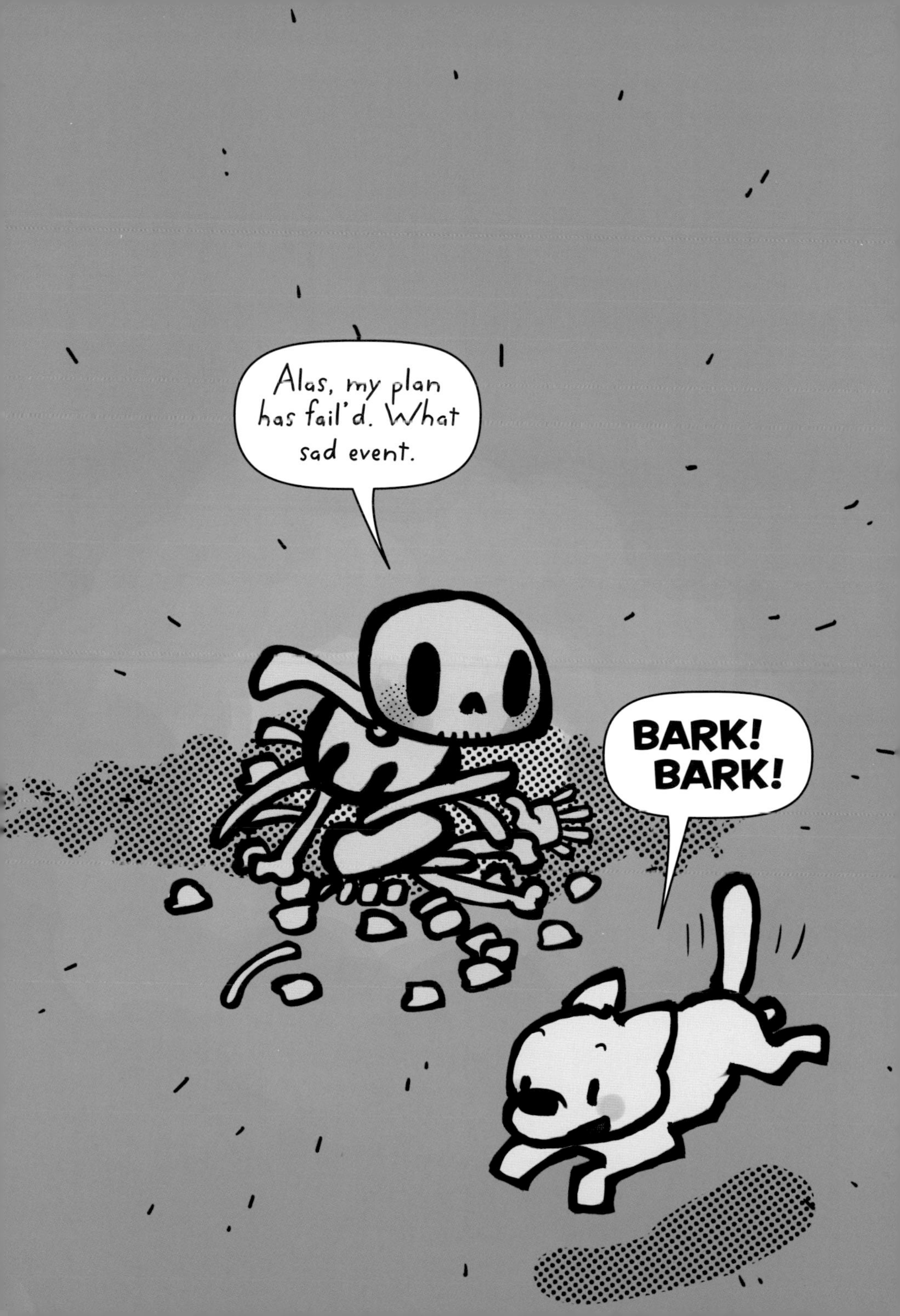
Alas, my plan has fail'd. What sad event.
BARK! BARK!

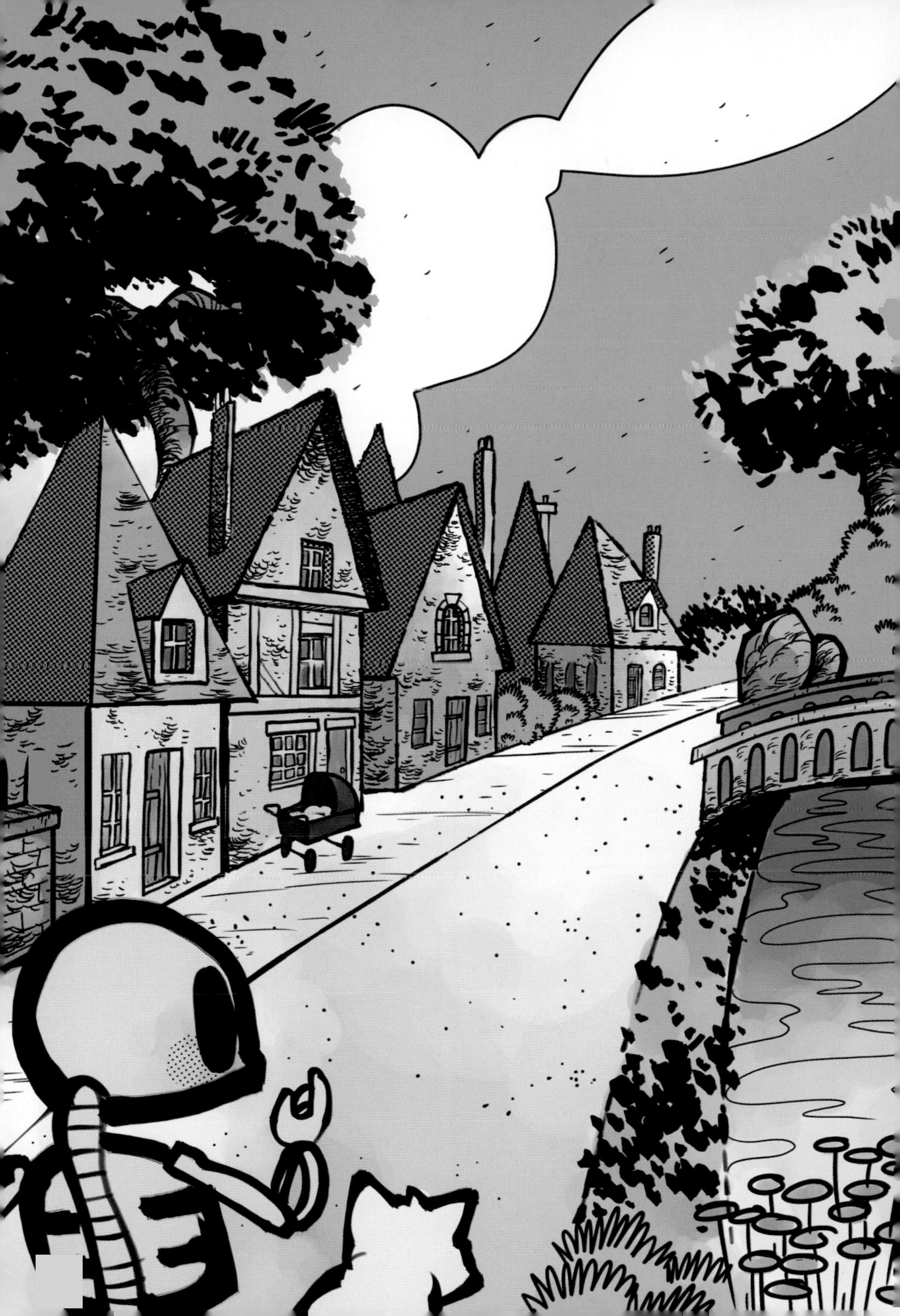

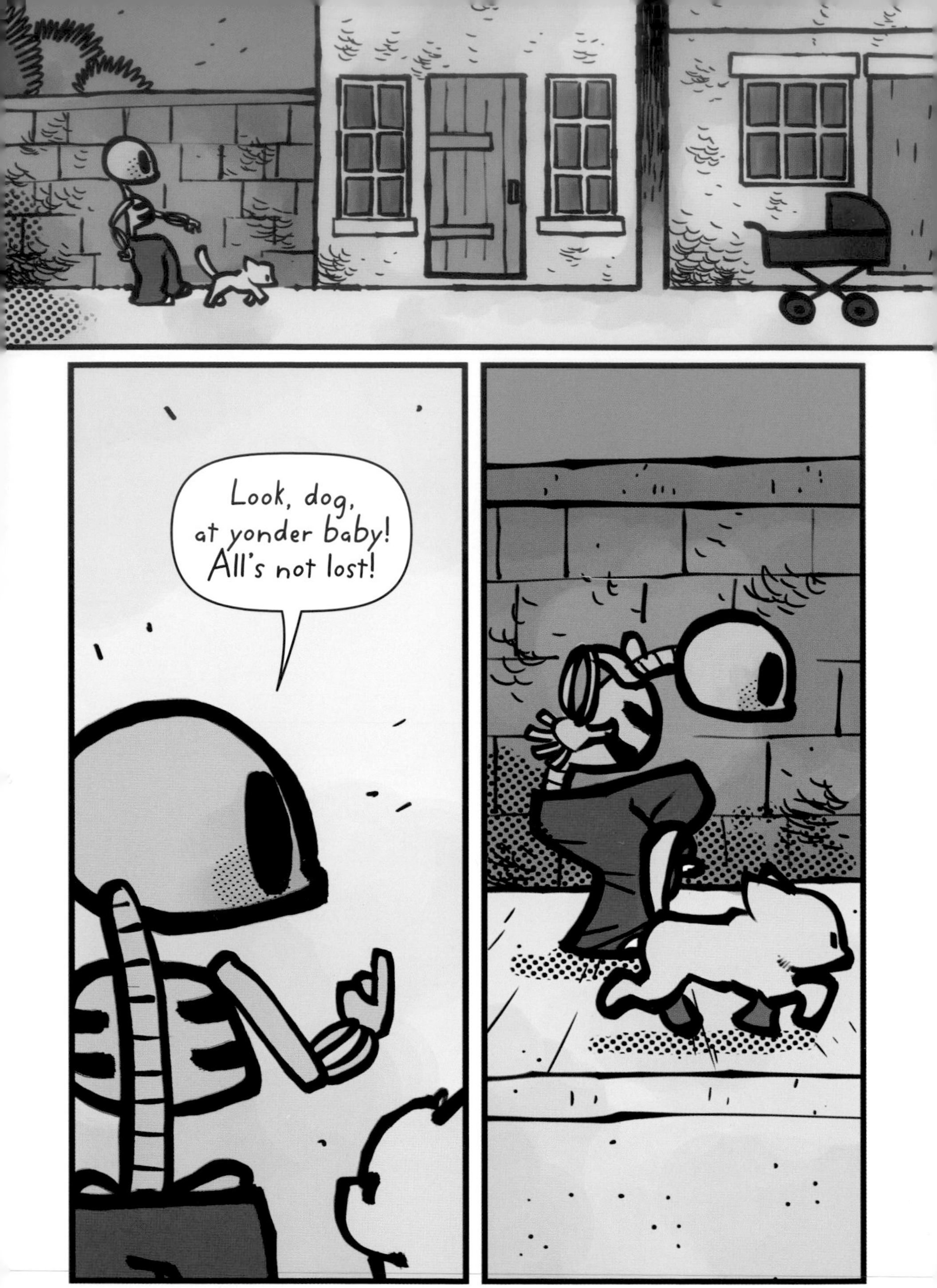
Look, dog, at yonder baby! All's not lost!

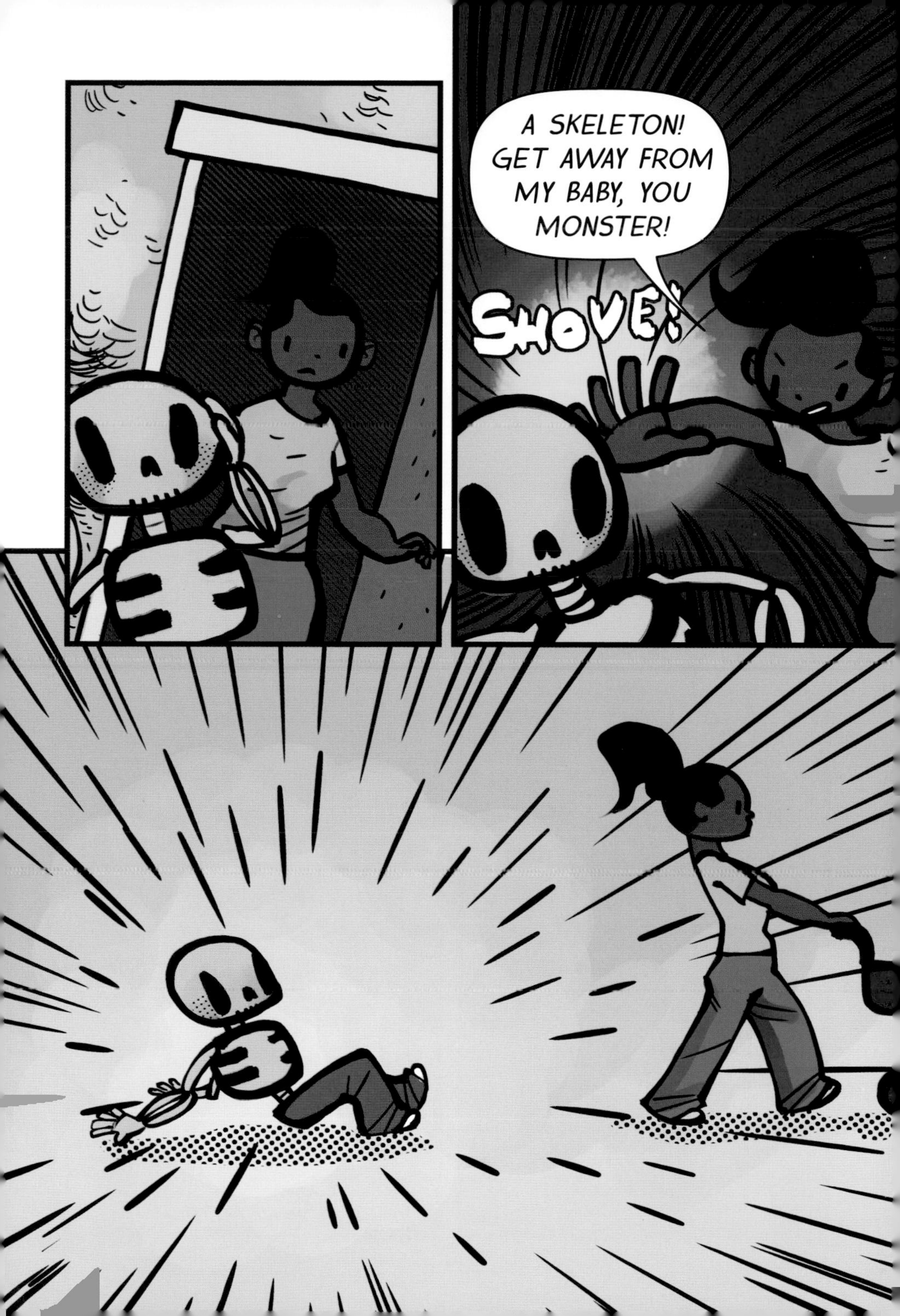
A SKELETON! GET AWAY FROM MY BABY, YOU MONSTER!
SHOVE!

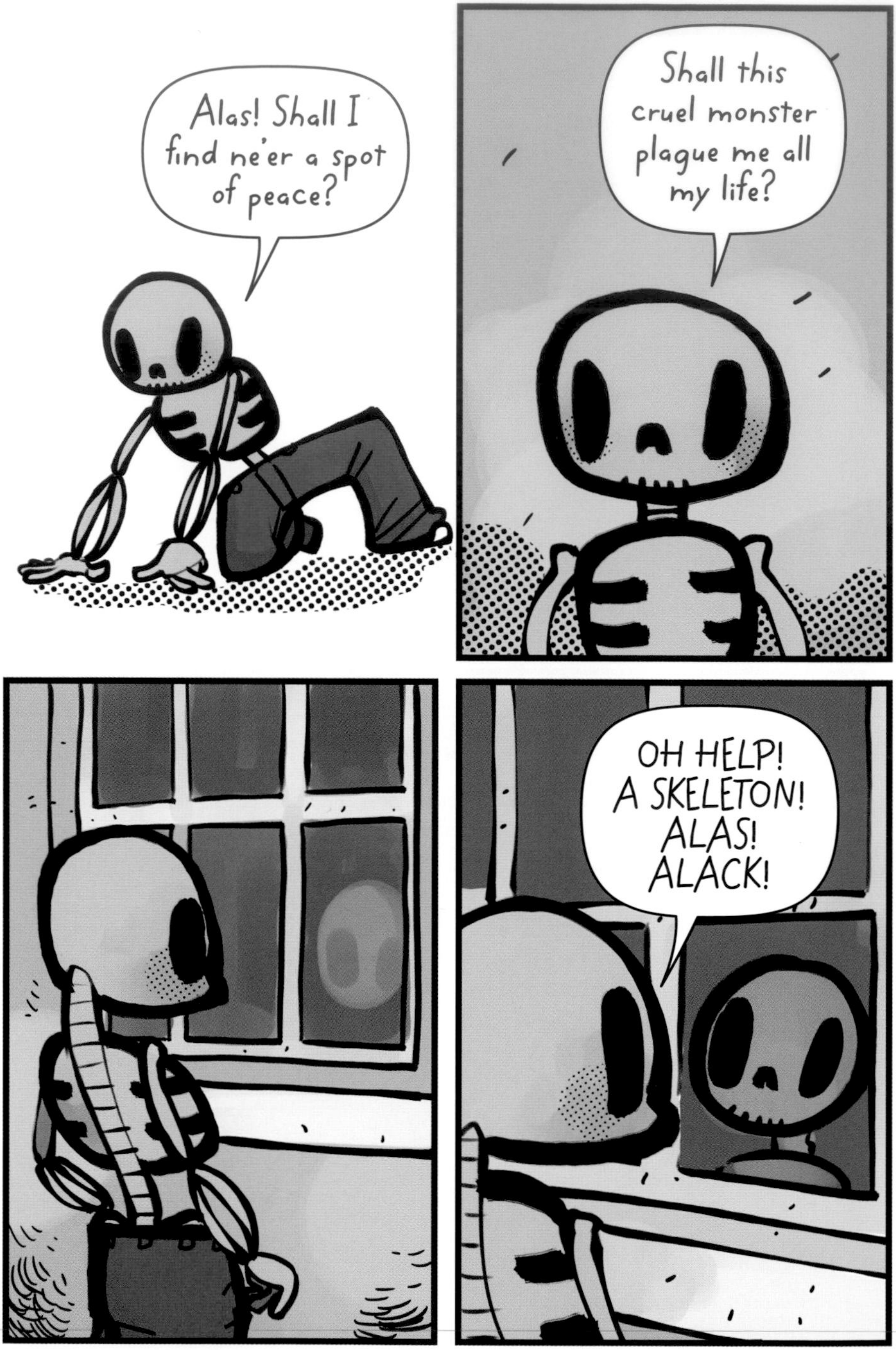
Alas! Shall I find ne'er a spot of peace?
Shall this cruel monster plague me all my life?
OH HELP! A SKELETON! ALAS! ALACK!

That boy who screamed in terror... Was't for me?
Did those girls not look at me and scream,
Pronouncing my condition? Verily,
I am the reason why I have no friends.

Ne'er shall I have my heart's desire: A friend—
For who could e'er love one so fear'd as me?
I am a monster, verily, I am,
And so shall live in solitude e'ermore.
Or, indeed, I shall not live alone. I do not live at all. I'm just alone.
LICK

I think it's best that we have flown so far
From human places. Ne'er again shall I reveal my face or any part of me.
At least out here I shall no trouble be.

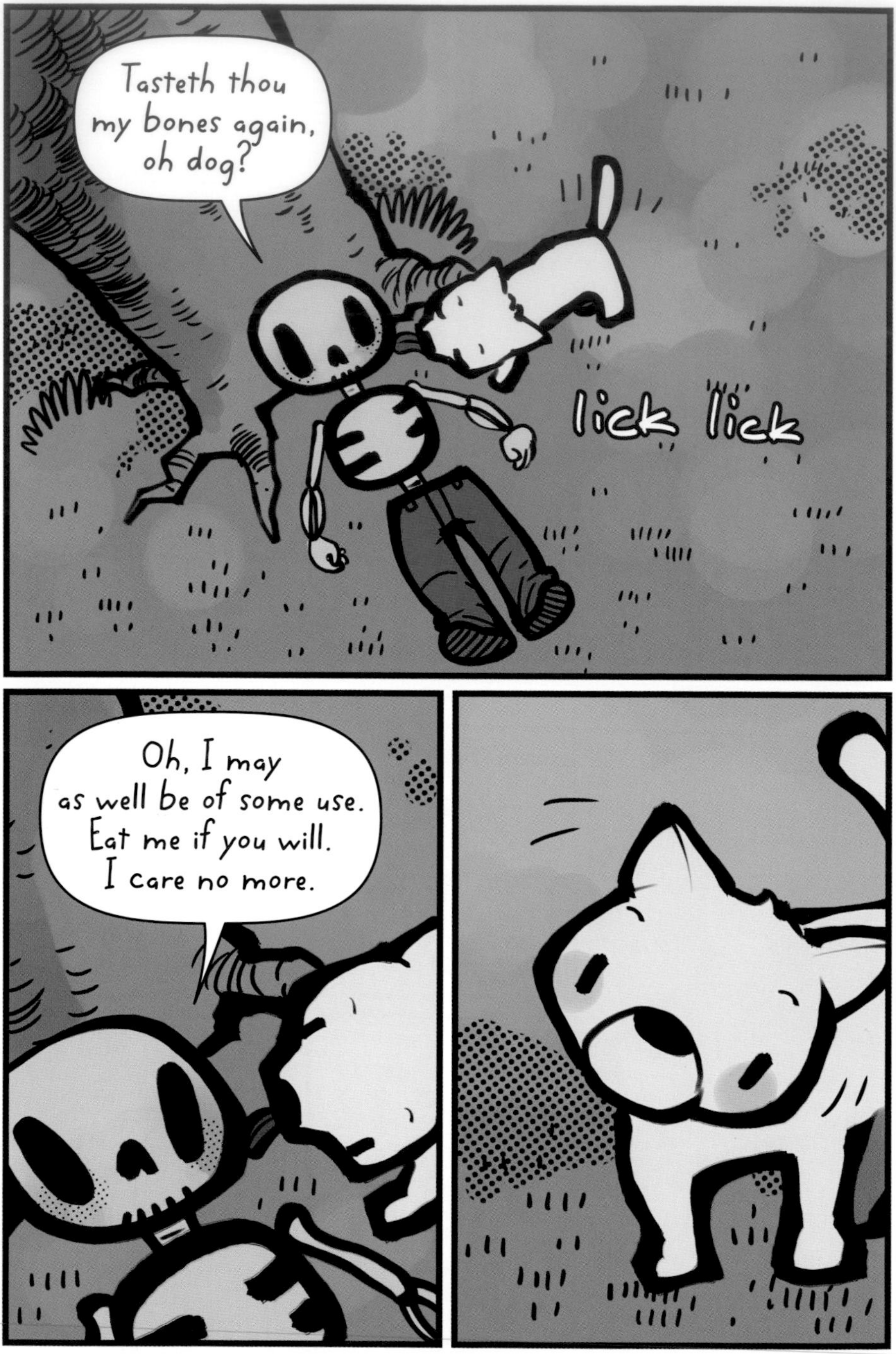
Tasteth thou my bones again, oh dog?
lick lick
Oh, I may as well be of some use. Eat me if you will. I care no more.

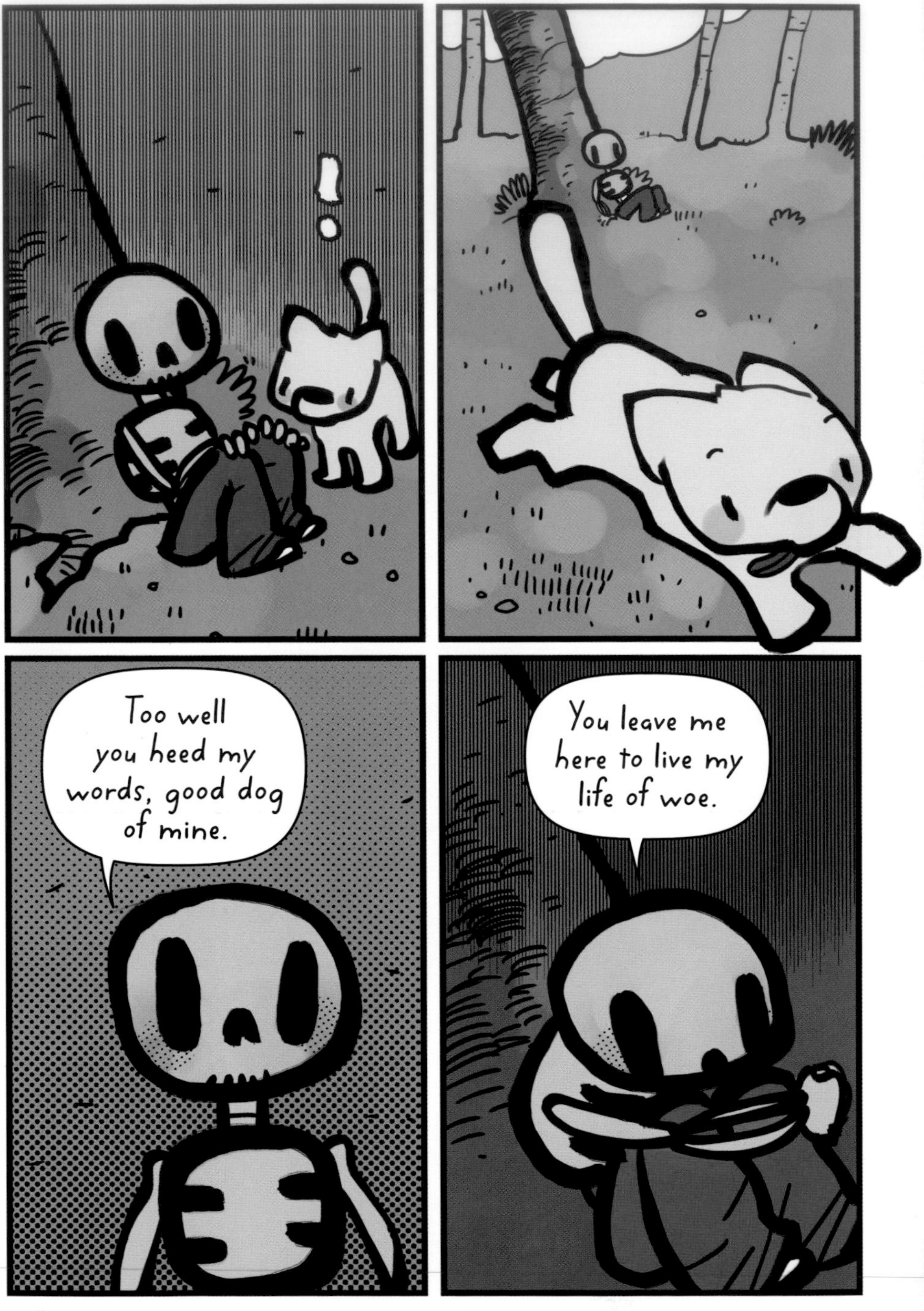
!
Too well you heed my words, good dog of mine.
You leave me here to live my life of woe.

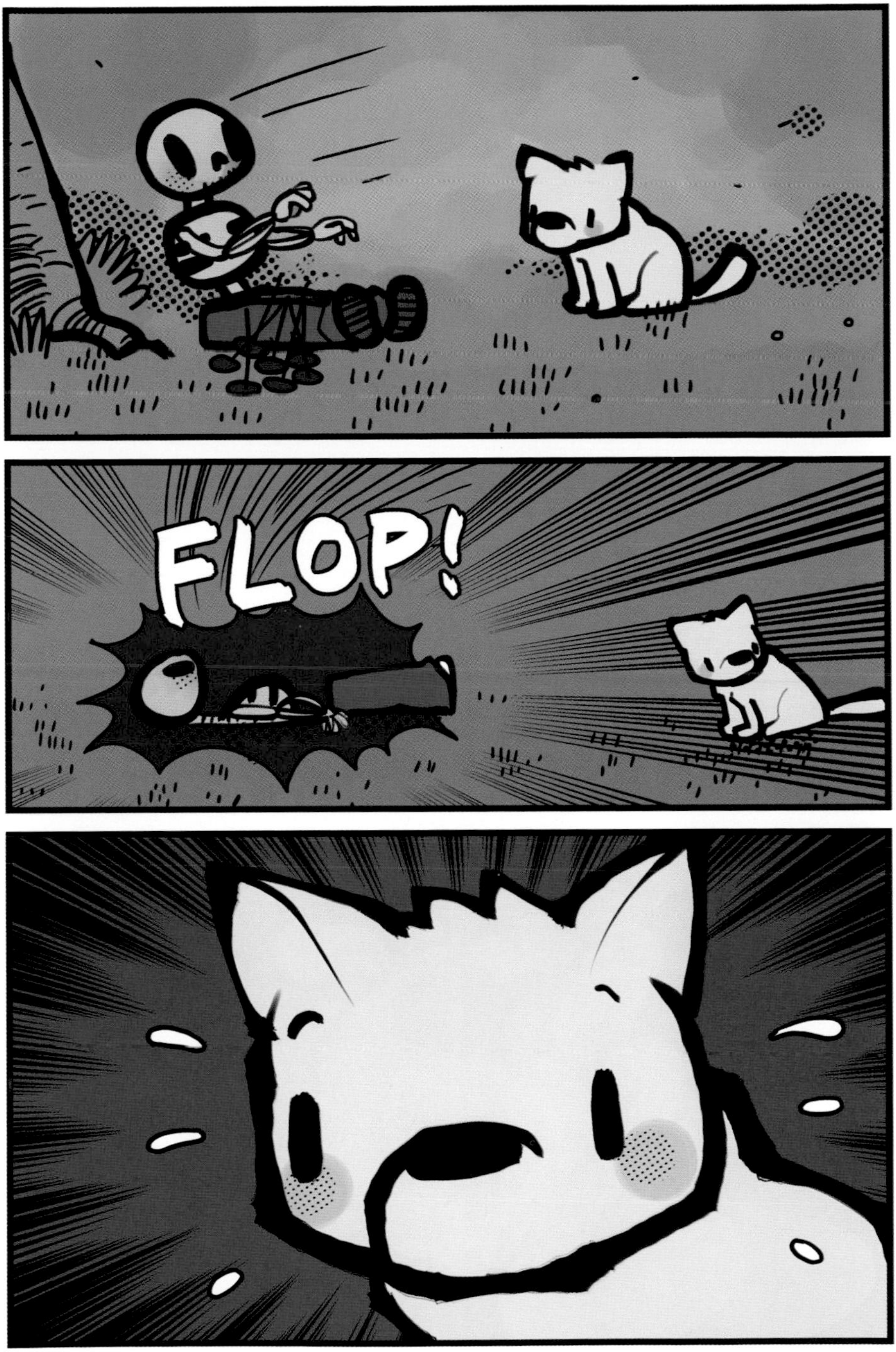
FLOP!

Oh goodness, dog, dost thou indeed know not...
...that life need not be e'er about thy needs?
Sometimes people want to be alone And dwell in misery within the grass.
'Tis easier by far to be upset When thou dost not try hard to cheer me up.

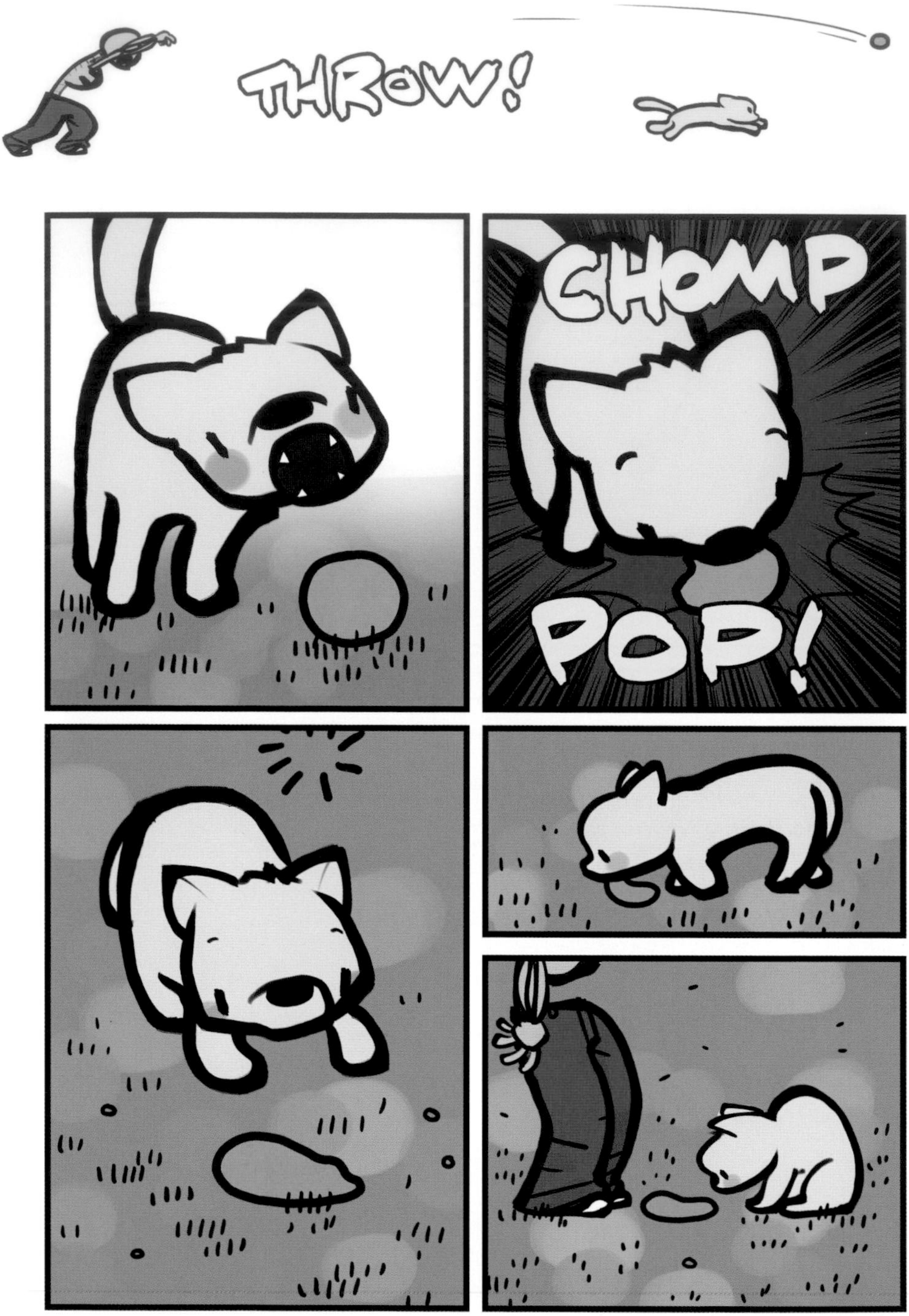
THROW!
CHOMP
POP!

Mayhap if I perform'd more vigrously...
SHIMMY SHIMMY
SHAKE SHAKE
SHIMMY SHAKE

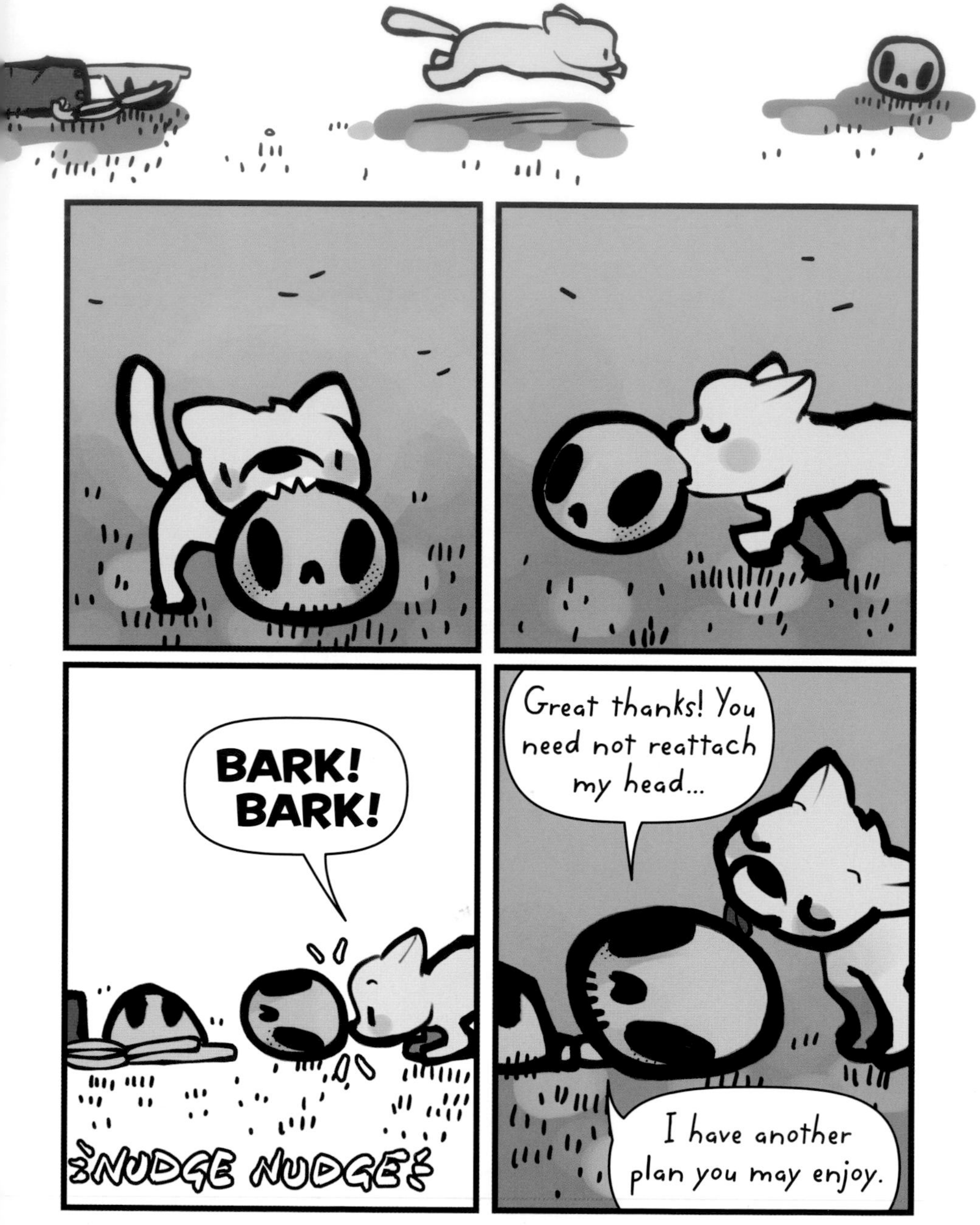
BARK! BARK!
NUDGE NUDGE
Great thanks! You need not reattach my head...
I have another plan you may enjoy.

Thou dost surely think, "What could be better than a ball?" Doth I divine this well?
Ne'er could I do this when I was alive.
This may be fun!
Art thou preparèd yet?

Come on, my lucky canine. Go on...
FETCH!
FLING!
Verily, the air doth cool mine face!

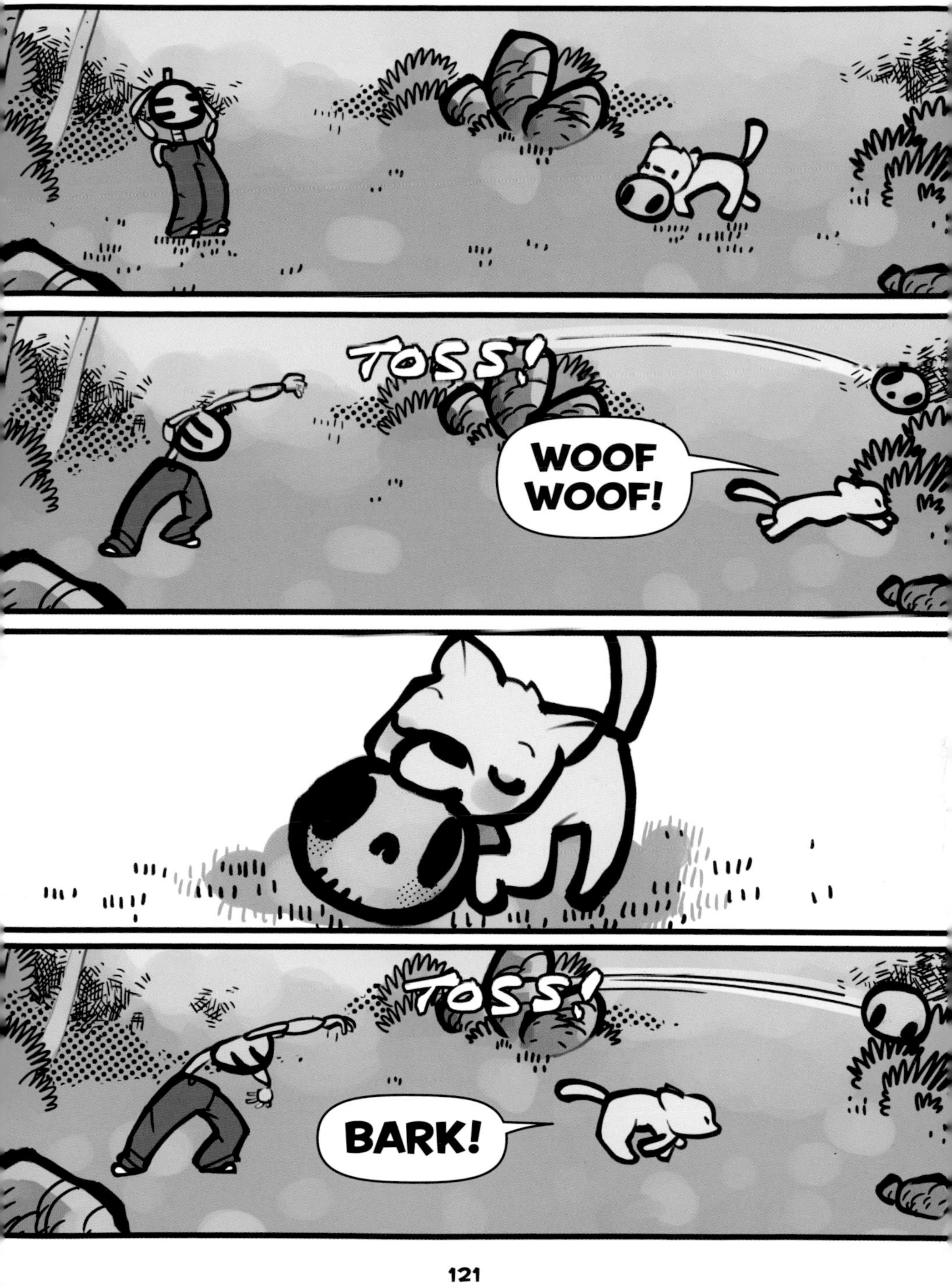
TOSS!
WOOF WOOF!
TOSS!
BARK!

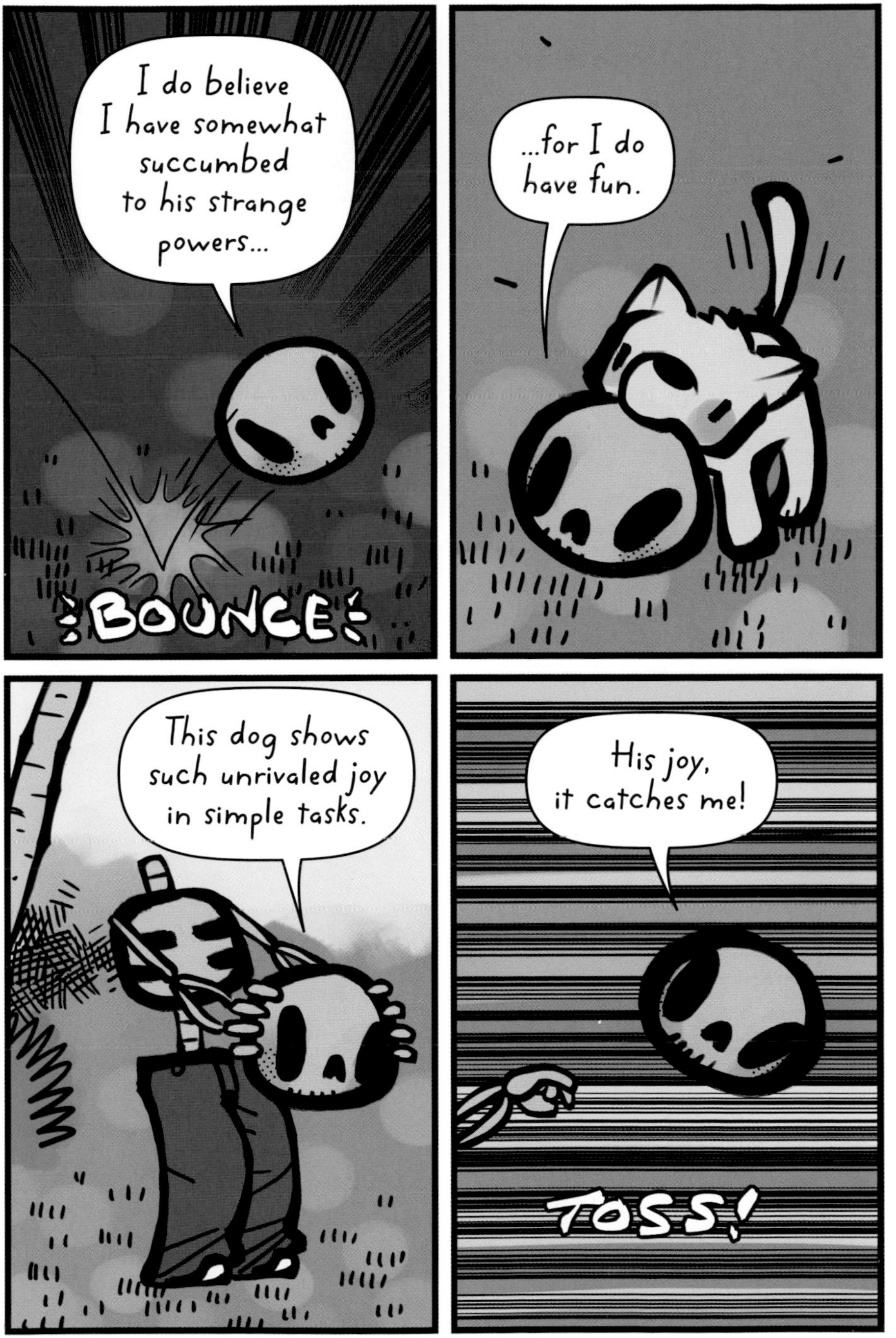
I do believe I have somewhat succumbed to his strange powers...
BOUNCE!
...for I do have fun.
This dog shows such unrivaled joy in simple tasks.
His joy, it catches me!
TOSS!

This small animal desired once To feast on my old sorry bones, yet suddenly...
He tries to cheer me up. He cares for me!
He'd rather that I live than be his food!
He wants me not to be left underground.
SPIN SPIN

I've realized of late, my dog, a truth: I wanted a companion, and I found thee!
Thou wast ne'er afraid of me, and lov'd me No matter what horrific thing was I!
How have I been blind to all of this?
You've been my friend since first you dug me up!

So, mutt, what's next? What shall we do together?
If we be friends, thou dost require a name.
What shall I name thee? Shall I name thee Puck?
No. Or Calaban? I thinketh not!
Rosencrantz? No, he's too strange a man.
Romeo? Alas, too tragic is't!

As I lay buried for so many years, I gradually forgot my distant past.
The passage of my time— mark'd with no tears. But sorrow— for eternity did last.
The world hath turn'd around without me there...
And I grew very lonely in those ages.

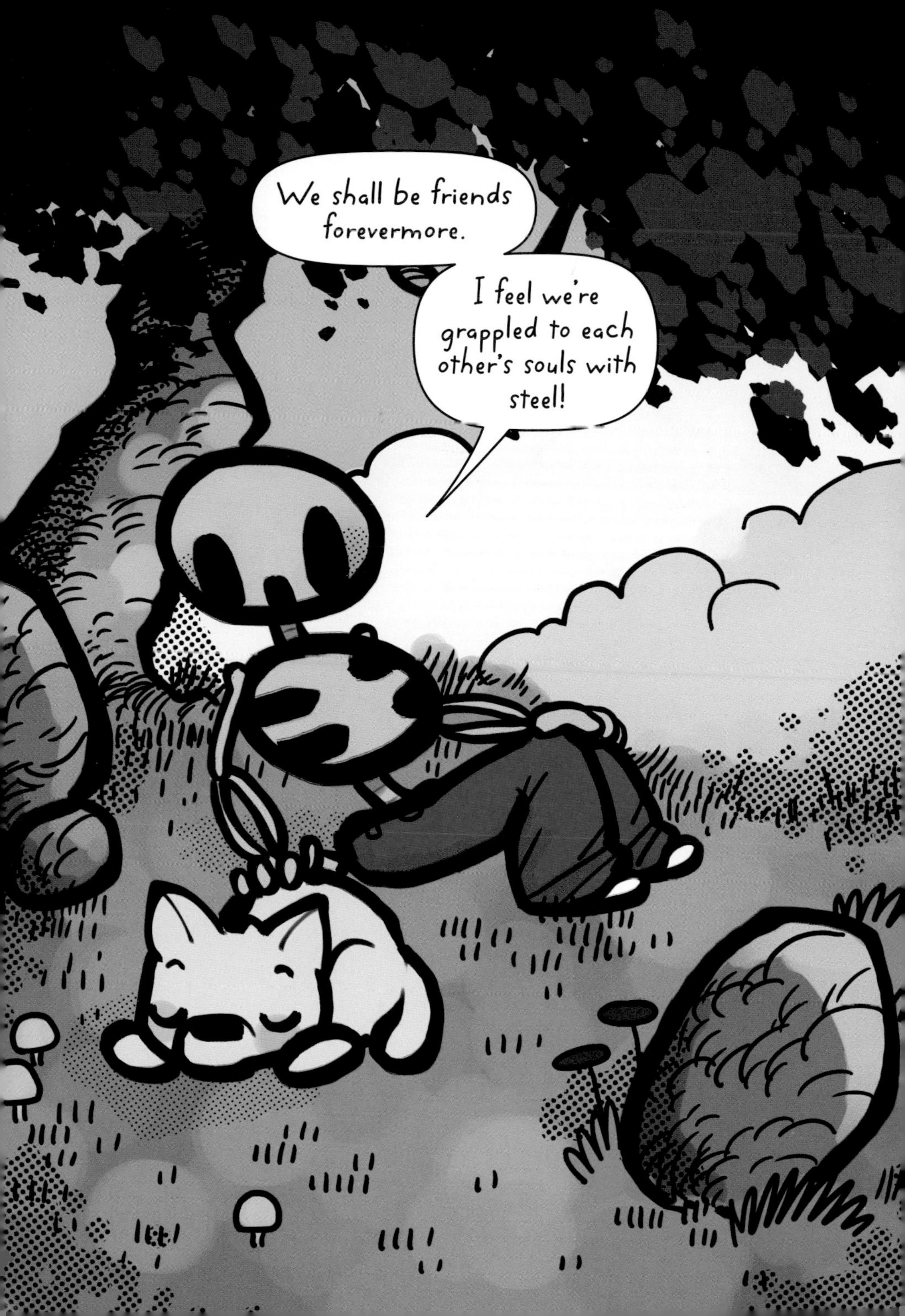
We shall be friends forevermore.
I feel we're grappled to each other's souls with steel!

Acknowledgments

Jeremy

This book has been the recipient of much love in its almost nine-year creation. It actually began life when I was seven years old. I drew a skeleton being terrorized by a small dog who wanted to eat him. Many years later I showed this drawing to some children during a school visit and suddenly realized there was a story to tell here! I came home and began writing and drawing a picture book. This picture book eventually became the graphic novel you now hold in your hands. It could not have made it to this point without a LOT of help. I especially wish to thank my agent, Holly McGhee, who, after years of reading my rewrites, suggested I hand the project over to Hermione, then only fifteen years old, and see what she could do with it. Holly had read a short Shakespearean script that Hermione had written and saw a spark of something amazing. The resulting script, along with some sample art, wound up in the hands of Andrew Eliopulos, who edited everything you just read and helped me hone this story into a real live book. I also owe a debt of gratitude to Erin Fitzsimmons and David Curtis for their expert art direction and design, and to everyone at HarperCollins Children's Books for getting behind this unique project. And, most important, to Hermione, for agreeing to take a stab at translating her dad's script into Shakespearean iambic pentameter, thus giving voice to Yorick. What an extraordinary partner to collaborate with! There's also my good friend Pat Sarell, who has been an enthusiastic supporter and encourager and sounding board. And finally, I must thank my wife, Heather, and my son, Theo, for their enthusiasm and encouragement for all my books. And, of course, you, dear reader, for coming along for the ride. Thank you.

Hermione

I am so grateful to my dad, the creator of this project, for letting me tag along on something that he's been working on for so long! This truly has been a journey, however, and so I feel that I should put my acknowledgments in chronological order. I would like to first thank my mom, without whom there would be no me. Jumping ahead a few years, I would like to thank Susanne and Paul Moniz de Sà, who directed the theater program I was in. They have taught me so much about theater and about life, and I believe it was Paul who first taught me about the rhythmic structure of Shakespeare's plays. So, thank you to Paul and Susanne. Next, I would like to thank Holly McGhee for looking at one of my creative projects, a rewrite of my dad's *Grumpy*

Bird in iambic pentameter, and encouraging me to use this weird skill! Thank you, of course, to Andrew Eliopulos for the amazing feedback and editing and pointing out of things that I would not have otherwise considered, and to everyone at HarperCollins. You really made this book what it is! Thank you, of course, to my dad for letting me be a part of his work. I have admired my dad's books since *Grumpy Bird* came out, and it is such an honor to be able to collaborate with him on this. Thank you to Ian Doescher, Adam Long, Daniel Singer, and Jess Winfield—some fellow writers/Shakespeare nerds who are a huge inspiration to me. Thank you endlessly to my mom, Heather, my brother, Theo, and all my wonderful friends for being so amazing and supportive and just honestly the best. And finally, thank you for reading this book! I hope you liked it!

Early Development of *Yorick and Bones*

I did this drawing when I was seven years old. I spelled "WOOF" wrong.

As I began work on *Yorick and Bones*, my early design for Yorick was fairly similar to my childhood drawing. I opted to keep adult proportions for Yorick. This changed later in the process because I decided smaller proportions worked better. When Hamlet talks to Yorick's skull in Shakespeare's play, he doesn't make it clear whether Yorick is a grown-up or not. I decided that Yorick was Hamlet's childhood friend.

Bones provided more challenging design problems than Yorick. What sort of a dog was he going to be? What color? Would he be anthropomorphic, wearing human clothes? All I knew was that I wanted him to be a small dog. And cute.

More drawings of Bones. When I'm uncertain about designs, I often fall back on a more highly rendered style—somewhat more realistic. This helps me see the "real" picture before I begin simplifying toward a final design.

More Yorick drawings. I had originally thought I would draw the whole book with a brush and ink. Some hand/wrist issues necessitated switching to digital tools. While I missed working with ink, I have no regrets. I think the digital art looks fantastic—it's nice and clean.